Agatha Raisin
AND THE
DAY THE
FLOODS
CAME

Agatha Raisin

AND THE

DAY THE FLOODS CAME

M.C. Beaton

CONSTABLE • LONDON

CONSTABLE

First published in the USA in 2002 by St. Martin's Press

This edition published in Great Britain in 2010 by Constable
Copyright © M. C. Beaton, 2002, 2010

5 7 9 10 8 6

A CIP catalogue record for this book
is available from the British Library.

ISBN 978-1-84901-145-7

Typeset in Palatino by Photoprint, Torquay
Printed and bound in Great Britain by
CPI Group (UK) Ltd, Croydon, CR0 4YY

Papers used by Constable are from well-managed forests
and other responsible sources

MIX
Paper from
responsible sources
FSC® C104740

Constable
is an imprint of
Little, Brown Book Group
Carmelite House
50 Victoria Embankment
London EC4Y 0DZ

An Hachette UK Company
www.hachette.co.uk

www.littlebrown.co.uk

Acknowledgements

The author wishes to thank Sue Quinn of the Go Places travel agency in Evesham and her assistants, Lynette James and Sonia Keen, for getting her, along with Agatha, to Robinson Crusoe Island.

The author also wishes to thank Pilates instructor Rosemary Clarke of Evesham, for all her help.

AGATHA RAISIN

Agatha Raisin was born in a tower block slum in Birmingham and christened Agatha Styles. No middle names. Agatha had often longed for at least two middle names such as Caroline or Olivia. Her parents, Joseph and Margaret Styles, were both unemployed and both drunks. They lived on benefits and the occasional bout of shoplifting.

Agatha attended the local comprehensive as a rather shy and sensitive child but quickly developed a bullying, aggressive manner so that the other pupils would steer clear of her.

At the age of fifteen, her parents decided it was time she earned her keep and her mother found her work in a biscuit factory, checking packets of biscuits on a conveyer belt for any faults.

As soon as Agatha had squirreled away enough money, she ran off to London and found work as a waitress and studied computing at evening classes. But she fell in love with a customer at the restaurant, Jimmy Raisin. Jimmy had curly black hair and bright blue eyes and a great deal of charm. He seemed to have plenty of money to throw around. He wanted an affair, but besotted as she was, Agatha held out for marriage.

They moved into one room in a lodging house in Finsbury Park where Jimmy's money soon ran out (he would never say where it came from in the first place). And he drank. Agatha found she had escaped the frying pan into the fire.

She was fiercely ambitious. One night, when she came home and found Jimmy stretched out on the bed dead drunk, she packed her things and escaped.

She found work as a secretary at a public relations firm and soon moved into doing public relations herself. Her mixture of bullying and cajoling brought her success. She saved and saved until she could start her own business.

But Agatha had always been a dreamer. Years back when she had been a child her parents had taken her on one glorious holiday. They had rented a cottage in the Cotswolds for a week. Agatha never forgot that golden holiday or the beauty of the countryside.

So as soon as she had amassed a great deal of money, she took early retirement and bought a cottage in the village of Carsely in the Cotswolds.

Her first attempt at detective work came after she cheated at a village quiche baking competition by putting a shop bought quiche in as her own. The judge died of poisoning and shamed Agatha had to find the real killer. Her adventures there are covered in the first Agatha Raisin mystery, *The Quiche of Death*, and in the series of novels that follow. As successful as she is in detecting, she constantly remains unlucky in love. Will she ever find happiness with the man of her dreams? Watch this space!

Chapter One

It was one of those grey days where misty rain blurs the windscreen and the bare branches of the winter trees mournfully drip water into puddles on the road as if weeping for summer past.

Agatha Raisin turned on the switch to demist the windscreen of her car. She felt that inside her was a black hole to complement the dreariness of the day. She was heading for the travel agent in Evesham, one thought drumming in her head. Get away ... get away ... get away ...

For miserable Agatha felt rejected by the world. She had lost her husband, not to another woman, but to God. James Lacey was training to take holy orders at a monastery in France. Sir Charles Fraith, always her friend and supporter when James went missing, had just got married, in Paris, and without even inviting Agatha to the wedding. She had learned about it by reading a small item in *Hello* magazine. And there had been a photograph of Charles with his new bride, a Frenchwoman called Anne-Marie Duchenne, small, petite, *young*. Grimly, middle-aged Agatha sped down Fish Hill in the direction of Evesham. She would escape from it all – winter, the Cotswolds where she lived in the village of Carsely, a broken heart and a feeling of rejection. Although, she reflected, hearts did not break. It was one's insides that got twisted up with pain.

Sue Quinn, the owner of Go Places, looked up as Agatha Raisin walked in and wondered what had happened to her usually brisk and confident customer. Agatha's hair was show-ing grey at the roots, her bearlike eyes were sad, and her mouth was turned down at the corners. Agatha sank down into a chair oppo-site Sue. 'I want to get away,' she said, looking vaguely round at the posters on the wall, the brightly coloured ranks of travel brochures, and then back at the world map behind Sue's head.

'Well, let's see,' said Sue. 'Somewhere sunny?'

'Maybe. I don't know. An island. Somewhere remote.'

'You upset about something?' asked Sue. In her long experience, unhappy people often headed for islands, unhappy people or drunks. Islands drew them like a magnet.

'No,' snapped Agatha. So deep was her misery, she did not want to confide in anyone and, in a sick way, she felt her misery still somehow tied her to James Lacey.

'All right,' said Sue. 'Let me see. You look as if you could do with a bit of sun. I know; what about Robinson Crusoe Island?'

'Where's that? I don't want one of those Club Med places.'

'It's in the Juan Fernández Archipelago.' Sue swung her chair and pointed to the map. 'Just off the coast of Chile. It's where Alexander Selkirk was marooned.'

'Who's he?'

'He was a Scottish seaman who was marooned there and Daniel Defoe learned about him and wrote *Robinson Crusoe* based on his adventures.'

Agatha scowled in thought. She had read *Robinson Crusoe* in school. She couldn't remember much about it except it conjured up a vision of remoteness, of coral beaches and palm trees. She would walk along the beach and feel the sun on her head and get her life together.

She gave a weary shrug. 'Sounds okay. Fix it up.'

Three weeks later, Agatha stood in the hot sunshine at Tobalaba Airport in Santiago and stared at the small Lassa Airlines plane which

3

was to carry her to Robinson Crusoe. There were only two other passengers: a thin, bearded man, and a young pretty girl. The pilot appeared and told them to climb on board. The girl sat in the co-pilot's seat and Agatha and the bearded man on one side of the plane. The other side was laden with a cargo of toilet rolls and bread rolls. Agatha's luggage, as per instructions, was limited to one travel bag. But the temperature in Santiago had been a hundred degrees Fahrenheit, so she had only packed underwear and light clothes. Her lunch was in a paper bag: one can of Coke, one sandwich and a packet of potato crisps.

The plane took off. Agatha gazed down at the vast sprawl of Chile's capital city and then at the arid peaks of the Andes. Then, as they headed out over the Pacific, her eyelids began to droop and she fell asleep. She awoke an hour later. She knew it was no use trying to talk to her fellow passengers because she didn't speak Spanish and they didn't speak English. There was nothing to see but miles and miles of ocean. She shifted miserably in her seat and wished she had brought a book to read. The pilot had a newspaper spread over the controls. She hoped he knew where he was going.

And then, suddenly, after another two hours of flying over the seemingly endless ocean and just when Agatha was beginning to think they would never arrive, there was Robinson Crusoe Island. Boo! It seemed to rear up out of the sea in front of them, black and jagged, as if the Pacific had just thrown it up. The small plane chugged towards a cliff, closer and closer. What's happening? thought Agatha as the plane appeared to start heaving its way up the cliff face. He's not going to make it. But with a sudden roar the plane lifted up and over the cliff top and came to land on an airfield. No airport buildings, no control tower, just a flat cliff top of dusty red earth.

It turned out the pilot had some English. Agatha gathered they were to walk down to a boat and the luggage and cargo would be taken down separately. She could feel gooseflesh rising on her arms. It was cool though sunny. Like a good Scottish summer's day in the Highlands. Agatha did not grasp she had moved into a subtropical zone. She only knew that she should have packed a sweater. The pretty girl who had been one of her fellow passengers indicated the road they were to take, and, with the bearded man, they walked across the airfield of dry red earth where locusts flittered in front of them like so many pieces of blown tissue paper.

The road curved down and down. The Jeep with the cargo and luggage roared past them. 'Bastards,' muttered Agatha, who was a strictly five-star-hotel traveller. 'They might have given us a lift.'

Just when her legs were beginning to ache with all the walking, she saw the sea below, a cove and a launch bobbing at anchor. Seals floated on their backs in the green-and-blue water. Hundreds of seals. There were already people waiting on the jetty, all young men carrying backpacks. Agatha, when she was miserable, liked to be fussed over and cosseted. When the luggage was stowed and they climbed on board and were given life jackets and told to sit on the hatches, Agatha suddenly wished she had stayed at home.

'You English?' asked a tall hiker type.

'Yes,' said Agatha, grateful to be able to speak after such an enforced silence. 'How long until we get there?'

'About an hour and a half. You could have gone by road, but it's pretty rough.'

'Everything seems pretty rough,' remarked Agatha. Above her, black mountains and sheer cliffs soared up to the blue sky. No beaches. Nothing but barren rock. A great setting for a horror movie or a movie about aliens. Amazing, thought Agatha, how, because of satellite television, one forgot that the world was really still a large place.

'I thought it would be tropical,' she said.

'That's because Daniel Defoe set *Robinson Crusoe* in the Caribbean.'

'Oh,' said Agatha and relapsed into gloomy silence.

She brightened only when the launch cruised into Cumberland Bay and she saw a small township and trees and flowers. She turned to the hiker. 'Where is my hotel? The Panglas?'

'Over there. That red roof.'

'But how do I get there? It seems miles.'

'Walk,' he said, and he and his companions laughed heartily.

They disembarked at a quayside. The pretty little girl tugged Agatha's sleeve and led her towards a Jeep. 'We get a lift,' said Agatha with relief. But the relief was short-lived.

The Jeep set off up a mountainous dry river bed of a road, lurching and bumping, swinging round to hang off the edge of a cliff, and then plunging down a steep gradient and roaring up the other side almost at the perpendicular. I'll kill Sue when I get back, thought Agatha, and then realized with a little shock that from the airfield to this scary journey to the hotel, she had not thought of James once.

To Agatha's relief, the hotel was beautiful. There was a huge lounge with picture windows looking out over the bay. Her room was very small, but the bed was comfortable. Outside the lounge was a deck with easy chairs. She searched through her luggage and put on a T-shirt with a long-sleeved blouse over it.

She went out on to the deck and ordered a glass of wine from an attentive waiter. It was warm in the sun and the air was like champagne. An odd feeling of well-being began to permeate her body. What a strange place, she thought. She could almost feel the darkness lifting out of her.

Her spirits rose even further at dinner, when as a starter she was served with one of the biggest lobsters she had ever seen. She tackled it with gusto and then looked round at her dinner companions. The pretty girl was there, but not the bearded man. The central table was dominated by a large family, speaking in Spanish. They were made up of an obviously married couple, thin and athletic, with three children – beautiful little girls – a middle-aged woman, and a young man. To Agatha's right, a husband and wife sat eating lobster in silence. Some of Agatha's old misery crept back. She did not know any Spanish. She was marooned on Robinson Crusoe Island and condemned to silence for the rest of her stay.

The middle-aged woman, who had been casting covert glances at her, suddenly rose and came over to Agatha's table. 'I hear from the staff you are English,' she said. She had a plump, motherly face and little twinkling eyes. 'I am Marie Hernandez and I am here with my daughter and her husband and my son, Carlos. The hotel does not hold many guests. Perhaps we should all sit together?'

Agatha happily agreed. She joined the Hernandez family, as did the pretty girl, but the silent couple in the corner merely shook their heads and stayed where they were. All the Hernandez family, from Santiago, spoke

8

English, apart from the small children, and they translated for the young girl, who said her name was Dolores. They all said, like Agatha, that they had expected a tropical island. Marie said she had a spare sweater in her luggage and would lend it to Agatha.

Marie told Agatha that the island was a national park. Her son, Carlos, proceeded to give Agatha a lecture on the history of Alexander Selkirk. He had been a seaman aboard the *Cinque Ports*, a privateer, and he had complained all the way around Cape Horn about the accommodation and the food on board. When the ship reached Juan Fernández to take on fresh water, he had demanded to be set ashore with a musket, powder, and a Bible. But when he saw the captain was actually going to go ahead with it, Selkirk said he'd changed his mind, but the captain had had enough of the grumbling seaman and so he was left. Most castaways would have shot themselves or starved, but Selkirk was saved by goats, introduced by the Spanish, which he hunted down, using their skins for clothes and their meat for food. He survived for four years, until 1709, when his saviour arrived: Commander Woodes Rogers of the privateers, *Duke* and *Duchess*, with famed privateer William Dampier. When Selkirk returned to London, he was a celebrity.

Agatha, not used to making friends easily, found at the end of the meal that she felt as if she had known this family for a long time. Dolores seemed to be picking up words of English with amazing rapidity.

When Agatha finally made her way to bed, she glanced curiously at the couple who had not joined them. The woman was blonde, dyed blonde, but very attractive in a baby-doll way, and the man, dark and Spanish-looking. They were sitting side by side on one of the sofas in the lounge. The woman was whispering to him urgently and he patted her hand.

Agatha felt there was something wrong there. Perhaps the journey had made her tired enough to give her odd fancies. She went to bed and plunged down into the first dreamless sleep she had experienced for a long time.

At breakfast the next day, Marie said they planned to walk up to Alexander Selkirk's look-out. She indicated the silent couple. 'I'll ask them if they would like to go.' She approached their table and plunged into rapid Spanish. But it appeared the couple did not want to go.

They all went down the cliff steps from the hotel after breakfast, where one of the staff relayed two lots of them in a rubber dinghy over to San Juan Bautista, the only settlement on the island. '*High Noon*,' said Dolores who, it transpired, had an English vocabulary confined mostly to film titles. She looked down the wide and dusty deserted main street and they all laughed as she drew and twirled an imaginary pistol. They began to climb, first up shallow steps leading up from the township, then on to an earthen track. The stream below them was surrounded by several varieties of wild flowers. Then they entered the silence of a pine forest. Agatha's legs began to ache, but she felt she could not give up while plump Marie soldiered on and even the little girls showed no signs of flagging. On and up they went until Agatha stopped and exclaimed at a flash of red. 'What was that?'

'Hummingbirds,' said Carlos. They waited and watched. Green-and-red hummingbirds whirred about. There was something about the beauty of them that caught at Agatha's throat and she suddenly sat down on a rock and began to cry. They gathered around her, hugging her and kissing her while Agatha poured out the whole story of her divorce. When she had finished, Marie said, 'So you begin a new chapter, here on Robinson Crusoe Island. A great place for beginnings, no?'

Agatha gave her a watery smile. 'Sorry about that, but I feel miles better.'

'We'll have our packed lunches now,' said Marie comfortably, 'and take a rest. Before you arrived at breakfast, I was wondering about the couple that would not come with us. They are Concita and Pablo Ramon, also from Santiago. They are on honeymoon.'

'Something odd there,' said Agatha, un-

11

wrapping a sandwich. 'They don't look like a honeymoon couple.'

'No. She is very much in love with him, I think. But he looks at her as if he's waiting for something.'

'Perhaps he feels he has made a mistake,' volunteered Carlos.

They finished their lunch and though no mention was made of Agatha's outburst, she felt enfolded in a warm blanket of friendship and sympathy.

To get to the lookout involved a final climb up sheer rock.

Agatha and Marie said they would wait below with the children while the more athletic ones made the ascent. 'Are you Catholic?' asked Marie.

'No,' said Agatha. 'Not anything, really. I go to the village church – that's Church of England – because the vicar's wife is a friend of mine.'

'And your husband? Was he Catholic?'

'Before? No.'

'But I do not understand. How can he become a monk if he was divorced and not even Catholic?'

'He didn't tell them when he first went there.'

'But they surely know now.'

'Maybe because I am not a Catholic, they do not consider it to have been a real marriage. Let's talk about something else,' said Agatha quickly.

Marie's attention was taken up then with the children. Agatha looked out at the vast stretch of the Pacific and was hit by a sudden thought. What if James had not really planned to take holy orders? What if he simply wanted to be rid of her and had found the monastery a convenient excuse? They had gone through an amicable divorce. They had talked about safe things – village gossip, James's plans to sell his house, but not once had he discussed his new-found faith.

Like the rest of the guests, Agatha had only booked into the Panglas for a week. The following few days took on a dreamlike quality of fresh air and exercise. They went to Robinson Crusoe's cave, they tramped the hills, returning at night, happy and exhausted. There was something about the remoteness and strange beauty of the island that seemed to heal the past and restore courage.

In the evenings, Agatha found her eyes drifting over to the honeymoon couple. On the last evening, the new bride was flushed and animated and talking in rapid Spanish. Her husband leaned back in his chair, listening, his face expressionless, but with that odd waiting feeling about him.

The farewells were affectionate and tearful. Agatha and Dolores were going on a later

13

plane than the family. They exchanged addresses and promised to keep in touch. 'Sad,' said Dolores.

'Yes, sad,' agreed Agatha, 'but I'll be back.'

Agatha broke her journey home with a few days in Rio at a luxury hotel. But she found she did not enjoy her visit. The heat was immense and the humidity high. She took a trip up Sugar Loaf Mountain and then decided to explore no further. Among the tourist brochures in the hotel was one advertising a tour to see where and how the poor of Rio lived. What kind of people, wondered Agatha, would go on such a tour – to gawp at the unfortunate? It was with relief that she finally boarded a British Airways flight for London. She had booked economy. She was at the back of the plane. There was only one screen at the end of the cabin and so she could not see any of the movies, and during the night she shivered in the blast of freezing air-conditioning. She complained to a female attendant, who shrugged and said, 'Okay,' and walked on. Nothing happened. People struggled into sweaters, huddled into blankets, and no one but Agatha showed any desire to complain. Bloody British, thought Agatha, finally collaring a male steward. He glared at her and nodded. The plane finally warmed up.

In future years, Agatha thought, they will

have models of this hell-plane in a museum and people will marvel that humans actually travelled in such circumstances, rather in the way that they wonder at the cramped accommodations in old sailing-ships.

At Gatwick, there was no gate available for the plane and so they waited an agonizing time before they were herded on to buses on the tarmac. Agatha then began the long walk to collect her luggage. She began to feel that the plane had landed in Devon and they were all walking to Gatwick.

By the time she collected her luggage, she was in a blazing temper. But her temper dissipated as soon as she had located her car and had started to head home. She began to worry about her two cats, Hodge and Boswell. She had left them in the care of her cleaner, Doris Simpson, who came in every day to look after them. James was gone; Charles, too. Only her cats remained a permanence in her life.

It had been a night flight and she had been unable to sleep because of the freezing conditions. By the time she turned down the road in the Cotswolds which led to her home village of Carsely, her eyes were weary with fatigue. Her thatched cottage crouched in Lilac Lane under a winter sky. Agatha parked and let herself in. Her cats came to meet her, stretching and yawning and rubbing against her legs. She crouched down and patted them and then caught sight of herself in the long hall mirror that she had put up so that she could check her appearance before going out. She straightened up slowly and stared.

She noticed the grey roots in her hair, the dull skin and the lumpy figure and drew her breath in. How she had let herself go! And all over two useless men who weren't worth bothering about. She phoned her beauticians, Butterflies, in Evesham, to make an appointment for the following day. 'Rosemary is having a Pilates class,' said the receptionist, 'so she can't do you in the morning. It'll need to be the afternoon.'

'What on earth is Pilates?'

'It's a system of exercises for posture and breathing and it exercises every muscle in your body.'

'I'm interested.'

'She has a space in her workshop tomorrow morning. It's an introductory class.'

'Put me down. When is it?'

'Starts at ten and goes on until one.'

'That long! Oh well, put me down.'

Agatha rang off. She fed the cats and let them out into the garden and then carried her luggage up to the bedroom. Too weary to unpack or undress, she fell on the bed and plunged down into sleep.

In the morning, as she drove to Evesham, she began to regret booking in for the Pilates class. Agatha was the type who booked an expensive course at a gym, went twice, and then chickened out and so lost her money. Still, she had to do something.

'Upstairs,' said the receptionist. 'They're about to start.'

Agatha climbed up the stairs. Four women were struggling into leggings and T-shirts.

'Agatha!' said Rosemary, the beautician. 'Welcome back.'

'Home again,' said Agatha with a grin. Rosemary was a very reassuring figure with her creamy skin and glossy hair. There was something motherly about her that made women feel unashamed of their lumpy figures and bad skin. Something reassuring that seemed to say, 'Everything can be made better.'

The class began. After relaxation, the exercises seemed gentle enough but required fierce concentration. The exercises had to be combined with breathing and strengthening the stomach and pelvic muscles.

They finally took a break for coffee and biscuits. Rosemary began to tell the small group that Joseph Pilates had been interned in World War I and that was when he had developed the system of exercises. After the war he had gone to America, where he had set up classes next to the New York Ballet School. She broke off and took Agatha aside. 'I know you must be dying for a cigarette. You can nip downstairs and go through to the room at the very back.'

Agatha longed to be able to say she wouldn't bother, but the craving for nicotine was strong. She stood in the back room feeling guilty, but nonetheless lighting up a cigarette. Sarah, Rosemary's assistant, was working on someone in the next room.

A girl's voice said, 'I didn't want to do this. But Zak wants me to get a bikini wax before I'm married.' This was followed by a giggle.

'Don't marry him!' Agatha wanted to scream. She had a feeling of feminist rebellion. It was all very well to keep oneself as fit and beautiful as possible, but all this total removal of hair, so that one looked like a Barbie doll, Agatha felt was going too far. And what sort of fellow ordered his girlfriend to have a bikini wax? 'Thanks, Sarah,' she heard the girl say. 'I'd better go. Zak'll be waiting for me. He wants to make sure I've got it done.'

Agatha heard her leave. She had a sudden urge to see this Zak. She stubbed out her cigarette and went through to reception.

A young man was standing there, hugging a pretty blond girl. 'You ready, Kylie?' he said. With his dark good looks and the girl's blond prettiness, Agatha was reminded of the couple on Robinson Crusoe Island. She was snuggling up to him, but he had the same waiting feel about him as the man on the island.

She shrugged and went upstairs just as the class was resuming. When it was over, Agatha cheerfully signed on for ten lessons. She felt relaxed and comfortable and the exercises appealed to her common sense. Time to fight against old age. Strengthen the kneecaps and avoid kneecap replacements; strengthen the pelvic muscles and avoid the indignity of incontinence. She told Rosemary she would go for lunch and come back to get her face done. She took out her mobile phone and called the hairdresser and booked herself in for a late appointment to get her hair tinted.

By the end of the day, when she returned home with her hair once more glossy and brown and her face massaged and treated, she began to feel like her old self, her old pre-James self. The 'For Sale' sign had gone from outside his cottage. She wondered what the new neighbour would be like.

The next morning, Mrs Bloxby, the vicar's wife, called. 'You look great, Mrs Raisin,' she said. 'The holiday must have done you good.'

Agatha began to tell her about the family on Robinson Crusoe Island and how much she had enjoyed their company. As she talked, she realized that she had not once bragged to them about her skill as a detective.

'Have you heard from James?' asked Mrs Bloxby.

'James who?' asked Agatha curtly.

Mrs Bloxby looked at Agatha curiously.

Agatha, before she had left, had refused to talk any more about James.

But Agatha suddenly remembered Marie saying that James could not surely take holy orders as he had been married. The thought that James might just have said that to get off the hook was something she did not even want to contemplate.

'So what's been happening?' asked Agatha lightly. 'No crime?'

'No murders for you,' said the vicar's wife. 'Very quiet.'

'Who's bought the cottage next door?'

'We don't know. There's a newcomer to our ladies' society, a Mrs Anstruther-Jones. She's just moved into the village. She wanted the cottage but someone else got it first, so she bought Pear Tree Cottage ... you know the one, behind the village stores.'

'What's she like?'

'You can judge for yourself. There's a meeting tonight.'

'Meaning you don't like her.'

'Now, I never said that.'

'If you don't have a good word to say for anyone, you don't say anything. How's Miss Simms?'

Miss Simms was secretary of the ladies' society, an unmarried mother.

'Miss Simms has a new gentleman friend. He's in sofas.'

'Married, I suppose.'

'I think so. Listen to that. The rain is on again. It's been raining since you left.'

The doorbell rang. 'I'm off,' said Mrs Bloxby.

Agatha opened the door and found Detective Sergeant Bill Wong on the doorstep. 'Hello,' said Mrs Bloxby. 'See you tonight, Mrs Raisin.'

'I thought you women would be on first-name terms by now,' said Bill, following Agatha through to the kitchen.

'It's tradition in the ladies' society that we use second names, and in this over-familiar touchy-feely world, I rather like it,' said Agatha. 'Coffee?'

'Yes. I see you haven't given up smoking.'

'Did I even say I would try?' demanded Agatha with all the truculence of the heavily addicted.

'Thought you might.'

'Never mind that. Here's your coffee. How's crime?'

'Nothing dramatic. Nothing but the usual cut-backs. Village police stations are closing down all round. Did you know they had closed Carsely police station?'

'Never!'

'Yes, and the one at Chipping Campden and the one in Blockley. So we spend most of our time on the road. Someone called nine-nine-nine last night and howled it was an emergency. Got there and found it was her cat stuck up a tree.'

'And how's your love life?'

'On hold.'

Agatha looked at him sympathetically. Bill had a Chinese father and an English mother, the combination of which had given him attractive almond-shaped eyes in a round face and a pleasant Gloucestershire accent. 'How's yours?' asked Bill.

'Non-existent.'

Agatha saw Bill was going to ask about James, so she began to describe her odd feeling about the couple on Robinson Crusoe Island.

'It sounds to me as if you were bored and looking for a bit of action, Agatha.'

'On the contrary, I wasn't bored at all. I met some super people. Still . . . there was something odd there. And I saw a couple in Evesham yesterday who reminded me of them.'

'You'd better find some work quickly or you'll be seeing crime everywhere. Thinking of doing any public relations work?'

'I might.' Agatha had once run a highly successful public relations company but had sold up to take early retirement and move to the country. Since then, she had often taken on freelance work. 'Public relations is a different world now,' she said. 'It used to be you were neither fish nor fowl. Despised by the journalists and the advertising people as if you weren't doing a real job. Now the public relations people are often celebrities themselves.'

'I hear Charles is married.'

'So what?'

'Oh, well,' said Bill hurriedly. 'I'd better get on. Let me know if you stumble across any dead bodies. I could do with a change.'

After he had left, Agatha switched on her computer to see if she had any e-mails. There was one from Roy Silver, a young man who used to work for her, asking where she was; and one from Dolores, the pretty young Chilean girl. To Agatha's dismay, it was all in Spanish, but she noticed the names Concita and Pablo Ramon. She printed it off and then drove to the Falconry Restaurant in Evesham, where the owner, Juan, was Spanish, and asked him for a translation.

'She says,' said Juan, '"Dear Agatha, Such excitement. Do you remember the couple, Pablo and Concita Ramon? Well, Pablo has just been arrested. It is in all the newspapers. Concita was drowned on Robinson Crusoe Island and Pablo said she fell out of the boat. But a hiker up on the hills saw him push her. He knew she could not swim. He had her heavily insured and her family are very wealthy. How are you? Let me know. Love, Dolores."'

So that's why he seemed to be waiting, thought Agatha. He was just waiting for the right opportunity. She wished now she had said something, let him know she was on to him. But she hadn't really noticed anything significant at all.

Agatha sat at the ladies' society meeting that night as Miss Simms, the secretary, in her usual unsuitable dress of tiny skirt, bare midriff, pierced navel and stiletto heels went through the minutes of the last meeting. The teacups clattered, plates of cake were passed round, and outside the rain drummed down on the vicarage garden. Mrs Anstruther-Jones turned out to be one of those well-upholstered pushy women with a loud braying voice. Agatha detested her on sight. She could feel some of her old misery creeping back again and tried the breathing exercises she had been taught and, to her amazement, felt herself beginning to relax. She would phone Roy and see if he had any work for her. James was gone and Charles was gone and Agatha Raisin was grimly determined to move on.

Chapter Two

Agatha found it hard, as winter moved into spring, to keep up her spirits. It was the rain – steady, remorseless rain. Water dripped from cherry blossom trees in the village gardens and yellow daffodils drooped under the onslaught.

And then in April, following a day of heavy cloudbursts, a watery sunshine gilded the puddles in Lilac Lane. Agatha set off for her Pilates class, to which she was now thoroughly addicted, the only healthy addiction she had ever had in her life. Just before the bridge on the Cheltenham Road in Evesham, she let out an exclamation of disgust. The police were diverting the traffic. She swung right. She was the leading car. Other cars followed her. If I make a left along here, she thought, it'll take me down to Waterside. She cruised down the hill and then jammed on the brakes with an exclamation of dismay. Waterside had gone. The river Avon was rising up the hill before her. She signalled to the other cars that she was going to reverse, made a three-point turn and decided to head out on the ring road over the Simon de Montfort Bridge and approach Evesham from the top road.

Cars were slowing over the bridge to look at the drowned fields on either side. She turned into Evesham and parked in the car park at Merstow Green. She decided to walk down to the Workman Bridge and view the extent of the flooding. She walked down Bridge Street, which is a steep hill leading down to the arch of the Workman Bridge. As she approached, she could see that Pont Street on the other side of the bridge was under water. Water surged past the houses on the waterfront. Two people outside Magpie Antiques were desperately hanging on to a doorway and waiting for help. Overhead, an Air Sea Rescue helicopter whirred across the sky. Agatha marvelled that the day had arrived when she could see Air Sea Rescue turning out to save the people of middle England.

She walked to the centre of the bridge and joined the spectators. Debris and tree branches raced past on the swollen river. There was a crunching sound as a caravan which had floated loose from a nearby caravan park got jammed under the bridge.

And then, as Agatha leaned over the bridge and stared down at the water, gilded by sunshine for the first time in weeks, she let out a gasp.

Like Ophelia, the girl from the beauticians,

who she remembered was called Kylie, floated underneath her on the flowing river. Her blond hair was spread about her. She clutched a wedding bouquet. As Agatha and the other spectators watched in horror, the body twisted and turned and sank from sight.

Agatha pointed and tried to scream, but as in a nightmare, no scream came out. But the other spectators were shouting and yelling. A policeman spoke into a two-way radio on his lapel and then, as they all waited, a police patrol boat came speeding along underneath. More policemen appeared on the bridge, saying, 'Move along. The bridge isn't safe. Move along.'

They were hustled back up Bridge Street by the police.

Agatha felt shaken. Zak did it, she thought. Just like that chap on Robinson Crusoe Island. All thoughts of going to her Pilates class were driven from her mind.

'You can't just barge in here every time you feel like it,' said Mrs Wong, barring the doorway to her home. 'I've read about women like you. Chasing young men.'

'I'm here on a police matter,' said Agatha, who had driven to the Wongs' home directly from Evesham.

'Then go to the police station. It's Bill's day off.'

Bill came round the side of the house at that

moment, holding a trowel in one earthy hand. 'Agatha!' he said. 'I thought I heard someone. Come round to the back garden. What about some tea, Mother?'

His mother muttered something sour under her breath and shuffled off. Agatha followed Bill. The garden was Bill's pride and joy. 'Just clearing up after that dreadful rain.' Bill indicated two garden chairs. 'Sit down and tell me what brings you.'

Agatha blurted out about the floods in Evesham and seeing the body of Kylie. 'She could just have been frightened by the prospect of her wedding and committed suicide,' said Bill. 'It'll come under Worcester police, not us.'

'He must have done it. Zak,' said Agatha. 'And remember I told you about that couple on Robinson Crusoe Island? Well, I had an e-mail from someone I met there and he did murder her. Said she fell off the boat but he was seen pushing her.'

'I would think it very odd if it turns out to be her fiancé,' said Bill. 'So obvious.'

'But isn't it usually the obvious?' asked Agatha. 'The nearest and dearest?'

'I've got a friend in Worcester police,' said Bill. 'I'll give him a ring tomorrow. Aren't these floods dreadful? And all those poor people with the contents of their houses wrecked by floodwater.'

'Terrible,' said Agatha vaguely, her mind still on that image of Kylie floating underneath her.

'I can't do much to help you until the police find out more,' said Bill. 'Meanwhile, let's go inside and have some tea.'

'I think I'd better get on my way,' said Agatha hurriedly. Bill's mother terrified her. 'If you've got a free moment in the next few days, drop over and let me know what you've found out.'

'If I can't manage, I'll phone you.'

When Agatha got home, she switched on the news. It was full of pictures of the flooded Midlands, tales of people being swept to their deaths, and then the announcer said, 'The body of a young woman was recovered from the river Avon at Evesham by divers. She had been spotted by onlookers on the bridge as she floated underneath. She was wearing a wedding gown. Police are not releasing her name until the family has been informed. So far, foul play is not suspected.'

'Pah,' said Agatha angrily. 'What do they know?'

Hearing her doorbell ring, she went to answer it. Miss Simms stood there, swaying slightly on her usual, very high heels. 'Can I come in?' she asked. 'I've got some news.'

'Of course you can come in,' said Agatha, leading the way to the kitchen. 'Is it about that girl in the river in Evesham?'

'What girl? No, it's about your new neighbour. He's John Armitage.'

'And who's he?'

'He writes detective stories. Ever so clever he is. Mrs Bloxby says his last one, *A Cruel Innocence*, was on the bestseller lists.'

'Married?'

'Don't think so. Mrs Anstruther-Jones said she once read an article about him in the *Sunday Times*. She's sure he's a widower.'

'How old?'

'About fifty-something.' Miss Simms giggled. 'Just the sort of age I like. I like mature men. They can be ever so generous, where the young fellows expect you to pay for everything.'

'When's he arriving?'

'Tomorrow.'

'Oh.' Agatha felt a flutter of excitement followed by a feeling of competitiveness. She must get to know him first.

'Anyway, what's this about a girl in the river?'

Agatha told her about the drowned Kylie. 'Are you going to find out who done it?' asked Miss Simms eagerly. 'I mean to say, maybe you and that new neighbour could join forces.'

'I don't suppose detective writers know anything about detecting,' said Agatha loftily.

But when Miss Simms had left, Agatha drifted off on a rosy dream. She and this John Armitage would solve the case together. 'Murder has brought us very close together,' he would murmur. 'I think we should get married.' And James would read about the wedding in the newspapers and feel terrible about what he had lost. She jerked herself out of her reverie to plan. First, she'd better get down to the bookshop in Moreton-in-Marsh and buy a copy of one of his books.

In the bookshop, all the talk was of the floods and how the main street at Moreton had been flooded. Agatha burst through the little knot of customers and interrupted their never-seen-anything-like-it exclamations to demand harshly, 'Any books by John Armitage?'

'Just his latest,' said the bookseller. '*A Cruel Innocence.*'

'That'll do,' said Agatha. 'Get me a copy.' And ignoring the glares of the interrupted customers, she paid for the book and headed back home. Once there, she unplugged the phone and settled down to read.

Her heart sank by the time she had read the first two chapters. The story was set in a tower block in Birmingham, much like the one in which Agatha had been brought up. It started with the ferocious gang rape of a young girl. It was compulsive reading, but Agatha read for escape, not to be reminded of scenes of her youth, the past which she tried so hard to forget about, to bury.

She began to picture this John Armitage in

31

her mind, for there was no photo of him on the cover of the book. He would be short with a beer belly. He would be middle-aged with a beard and a false hearty laugh. But she continued to read, because the story was gripping, and by the end of it she knew she was free from indulging in any romantic thoughts about her new neighbour. Let the other village women call on him with scones and cakes. She, Agatha Raisin, would get on with studying one real-life murder for Agatha *was* convinced it was murder.

Agatha drove down to Moreton-in-Marsh the next morning to buy the *Evesham Journal*. There were pages of photographs of the flood, but only a brief report about Kylie's death, still with that quote from the police saying that they could not release the name until close family had been informed. She returned home. A removal van stood outside the neighbouring cottage, but she only gave it one brief, sour glance before letting herself into her own cottage. She phoned Bill Wong at Mircester police headquarters but was told he was out on a job.

She then phoned Rosemary at Butterflies and asked for Kylie's address. 'I can't do that, Agatha,' said Rosemary. 'I wouldn't, for example, give anyone your address.'

'But she's dead and I'm not.'

'Sorry. Can't do it. You do understand?'

'No,' said Agatha crossly and put down the phone and then wondered what she was doing snapping at the best beautician around.

There was a ring at the door. When she answered it, Mrs Bloxby was standing there.

'Come in,' said Agatha. 'I've got lots to tell you.'

Over coffee, she described seeing Kylie's body in the river. 'It's so frustrating,' said Agatha finally. 'I'd like to get started but I don't know anything about her.'

'It's early days yet,' said the vicar's wife soothingly. 'You may have a soul mate next door.'

'Him! I read one of his books.'

'They are very violent but he does know how to tell a good story.'

'He doesn't seem like my type.'

'You've seen him?'

'Not yet. But you can always tell what they look like from their writing. He's probably short and fat with a beer belly and a beard.'

'My! And you got all that from just reading one of his books?'

'I'm quite good at that.'

Mrs Bloxby, who had just met John Armitage, opened her mouth to tell Agatha that she was way off the mark, but then closed it again. An Agatha in love once more with a next-door neighbour didn't even bear thinking of. Mrs Bloxby was fond of Agatha and did not want to see her getting hurt again.

'Well, I gather he's going up to London for a week immediately after he's unloaded his stuff, so you won't be able to see if your description fits for another week.'

'Not interested anyway,' said Agatha with a shrug, assuming the vicar's wife hadn't yet met the author either.

After a week, Agatha had quite forgotten about her neighbour and was wondering if she would ever be able to get in touch with Bill Wong again. She dreaded calling at his home and finding herself put down once more by the terrifying Mrs Wong. But just as she was wondering whether she should stake out Mircester police headquarters to see if she could waylay him, Bill called round.

Agatha practically dragged him into the house, crying, 'Where have you been? What's been happening?'

'Sit down. Relax,' said Bill. 'I got caught up investigating a series of break-ins in Mircester and only got round to phoning my friend in Worcester CID last night. It's all rather odd.'

'What's odd?' asked Agatha, scrabbling in a packet for a cigarette while not taking her eyes off Bill's face.

'She died of an overdose of heroin. Her fiancé, Zak Jensen, says she was addicted but she had promised him that she had given up the habit.'

Agatha's face fell. 'So it was suicide?'

'We might think so, except for one thing.'

'What's that?'

'The body had been frozen.'

'What?'

'Yes, after death the body had been frozen. It was dumped in the river during the floods. Maybe the idea was to give the impression that she was just another flood victim.'

'In her wedding gown!'

'Yes, you would think they would have taken it off first. But then it would have been frozen to the body. The girl's name was Kylie Stokes. She worked for a company on the Four Pools Estate. She was something to do with computers. Four days before her body was discovered, the girls in the office gave her a hen party, all getting drunk and dressing her up in tinsel and streamers and parading her through the streets. Her wedding was supposed to have taken place two days after. She had already taken leave from work. Her mother says she went out late and never came home. She reported her missing to the Evesham police. Every shop and building and home in Evesham that might have a deep freeze is being checked.'

'And what of Zak?'

'Well, as we can't pin-point the time of death, it's hard to ask him for an alibi for a specific time.'

'Bill, when I saw her at the beauticians, she did not look like a drug addict. She looked the picture of glowing health and happiness.'

'That's the most I can tell you at the moment.'

'What sort of family are the Stokeses?'

'No harm in telling you. It'll be in the papers tomorrow. Mrs Freda Stokes is a widow. Works a stall at Evesham Market, you know, the covered market in the High Street. By all reports, decent and hard-working. Kylie was her only child. This whole thing has hit her hard. She lives in one of those terraced houses near the income-tax office, just off Port Street. I haven't the number with me, which is probably just as well. She's very distressed, so I don't want you knocking on her door.'

'And what about Zak?'

'He's employed as a bouncer at his father's disco called Hollywood Nights in Evesham. The police have been called out to the disco several times, usually drunken fights between youths. Neither he nor his father has any criminal record. Zak seems genuinely broken up.'

'If she was in her wedding gown, you'd think if, just if, someone gave her an overdose of heroin that the murder would have taken place at her mother's house. I mean, the groom isn't supposed to see the bride in her gown until the wedding.'

'Agatha, if it weren't for the fact that the body had been frozen, I would be happy to

assure you that Kylie was just another unfortunate on drugs.'

'And wouldn't a frozen body have sunk?'

'No. On the contrary. If the body had still
been frozen, it would have floated. It had
thawed out to river temperature, which isn't
very warm, and the flood currents in the Avon
were strong. The police think the body got
caught in some sort of whirlpool just before
the bridge and spun up to the surface before
sinking again. But don't go around thinking
Zak did it. Just because there was a case in
Chile doesn't mean the same thing happened
here. Kylie's mother isn't well-off by any
means. Kylie hadn't made a will. There was
nothing to be gained by her death.'

'That disco. Are you sure there's nothing
there to connect it to drugs?'

'No, nothing. If there were, Worcester police
would know. I've said this before, Agatha, and
I'll say it again. Why don't you leave it all to
Worcester police this time? They really are
very good indeed.'

'Humph!'

After Bill had left, Agatha decided to drive
into Evesham and ask Sarah, who had been
working on Kylie, whether she thought the
girl had been on drugs. As she got in the car,
she saw a squat man with a beard working in
the front garden of the house next door. She

grinned to herself. He was everything she had imagined the author to be.

She parked in Merstow Green in Evesham and went in to the beauticians. She was in luck, Sarah had just finished with one customer and was taking a break before the next.

'I want to ask you about Kylie,' said Agatha. 'Did she look as if she was a heroin addict?'

Sarah looked shocked. 'No, she was the picture of health. Not only were there no track marks, but no signs that she had been sniffing the stuff. Beautiful skin that poor girl had. Is that how she died? Drugs? Was it a bad Ecstasy pill?'

'I gather the police are saying she died of a heroin overdose.'

'Oh, dear. There's a lot of drugs in Evesham, I believe.'

'Have you heard anything about that disco, Hollywood Nights?'

'Not a thing, but then I don't live in Evesham.'

Agatha thanked her and left. She stood outside, irresolute. As if to mock the recent suffering of the inhabitants, the weather had turned balmy and warm. She suddenly missed both James and Charles. They would have been every bit as interested as she was in finding out what had happened to Kylie. Then she thought of Roy Silver, who had once worked for her. She would invite him down for the weekend.

* * *

Roy descended from the London train at Moreton-in-Marsh wearing a black, sort of Gandhi-style collarless business suit and fake crocodile boots with very pointed toes. He came off the train talking rapidly into his mobile phone.

'You're impressing no one,' said Agatha as she went to met him and he tucked his phone away. 'Every nerd in the country has a mobile phone.'

'You haven't changed,' said Roy huffily. 'I do have a stressful job, you know.'

He still had the white-faced, rather weedy look of an East End of London urchin. He deposited a damp kiss on her cheek and then followed her to her car where he stowed his luggage in the back.

'So tell me all about this murder,' he said as Agatha drove off.

Agatha told him what she knew, ending with, 'If it wasn't for the fact that the body had been placed in a deep freeze somewhere, the police might have let it go as death by misadventure.'

'Still could be.'

'How do you make that out?'

'Well, say the fiancé knew about her drug habit. She doesn't need track marks. She could have been sniffing the stuff. She finally takes to the needle, drops dead. This Zak is alarmed. Doesn't know what to do. Panics. Puts the body in a freezer somewhere. The police can't find all the freezers in Evesham. Could be one in a shed in someone's back garden. A lot of these chest freezers are too big to keep in the house. Panic subsides. Realizes he should have left the body as is. Can't call the police. Floods start. Great opportunity. Dump it in the river.'

'But in her wedding dress!'

'Well, people in a panic will do anything. Where do we start, Sherlock?'

'I thought we might go to that disco tonight.'

'We'd stick out like a pair of sore thumbs. I can pass, but you're too old, sweetie.'

'Thanks a bunch.'

'So we need an excuse. I tell you what, I had a friend who was a researcher for the BBC. He said half his time was going places and asking people all sorts of questions. I'll be the researcher and you can be someone who's writing a script on the life of young people in middle England. Except for one thing: Hasn't your photo been in the local papers in the past?'

'Yes, but I can disguise myself.'

'Try and I'll see if you'll pass.'

Agatha called on Mrs Bloxby accompanied by Roy because there was a box of theatrical wigs and costumes at the vicarage, used for the various church amateur dramatic shows. Agatha selected a blond wig and a pair of spectacles with plain glass lenses. Once she had tied the wig back with a black ribbon, it looked less false.

'You'll do,' said Roy.

'I don't suppose you'll come to any harm,' said Mrs Bloxby doubtfully, who had been told all the latest news about the death of Kylie.

'Just going for a recce,' said Agatha cheerfully.

'Have you met your new neighbour yet?'

'No, but I've seen him and he's everything I imagined him to be.'

'Without talking to him?'

'I don't need to. I saw the beard and the beer belly.'

Roy noticed a look of almost unholy glee in Mrs Bloxby's usually mild eyes. At that moment, the vicar called from the study. 'That Anstruther-Jones woman is coming up the path. Has the Agatha creature left yet?'

'Excuse me,' said Mrs Bloxby, flushing pink. She hurried off to the study.

'The vicar doesn't seem to like you,' said Roy as the doorbell went.

'Oh, I don't think he likes anyone,' said Agatha huffily. 'In my opinion, he shouldn't be a vicar at all.'

The doorbell rang again.

'Should we answer it?' said Roy.

'Leave it to them,' retorted Agatha.

The vicar appeared, looking flustered, followed by his wife. 'My dear Mrs Raisin,' he said, 'I gather from my wife that you over-heard me referring to some Agatha creature. I am so sorry. We have a mangy stray cat around the churchyard called Agatha and my wife will feed it.'

Roy reflected that he had just heard one of the lamest excuses ever, but Agatha seemed mollified. The doorbell went again. 'I suppose I'd better answer it,' said Mrs Bloxby. The vicar hurried back to his study.

Mrs Anstruther-Jones bustled in. 'Oh, Mrs Raisin,' she fluted, 'and who do we have here? Your son?'

'No,' said Roy, straight-faced. 'I'm her lover.'

'Let's go,' said Agatha, gathering up her disguise.

'Well, I never!' exclaimed Mrs Anstruther-Jones after the door had closed behind Agatha and Roy. 'Disgraceful. A woman of her age! I hope, as a lady of the church, Mrs Bloxby, you told her what you think of her liaison.'

'Mrs Raisin is not having an affair with that young man.'

'But he said –'

'When confronted with someone who appears to be in a perpetual state of outrage, it is tempting for other people to wind them up. Besides, I have always found the most vociferous guardians of morality on matters of sex are those who aren't getting any. Some tea?'

* * *

Agatha recognized Zak, standing at the door of the disco. Whatever distress he might feel over the odd death of his bride-to-be did not show. He smiled and said, 'You sure you want to come in here? It's all young folks.'

'We're doing some research for a television programme on provincial entertainment,' said Agatha.

'Well, then.' Zak beamed and flexed his muscles under his dinner jacket. 'You've come to the right place. You'd better have a word with my dad. He owns the place.' He turned and shouted, 'Take over the door, Wayne.'

A thuggish young man came out. His beady eyes raked over Agatha and Roy. 'Police, again?'

'No, television,' said Zak proudly. 'Come along.'

The disco had the usual revolving crystal ball with strobe lights shooting at it from different corners of the room. Kylie must have thought she had won the jackpot getting Zak, thought Agatha. Some of the girls were pretty, but the youths were of the thin, white-faced, round-shouldered type, as if they had spent their formative years hunched up in front of the television set eating junk food. There was a bar over in the corner to which Zak led them. The music was so loud, it beat upon the ears, it reverberated through the floor under their feet, and it assaulted every sense. The air was hot and filled with the smell of sweat and cheap perfume. Zak's father was standing at the bar. Zak mouthed something in his ear and he looked at Agatha and Roy and then jerked his head. They followed him up a staircase at the corner of the room and then through a thick padded door and into an office. Agatha sighed with relief as the dreadful sound of the music became muted to a thud-thud-thud on the downbeat.

'I'm Terry Jensen,' said Zak's father. 'Sit down. Drink?'

Agatha asked for a gin and tonic and Roy ordered the same. Terry went to a glass-and-wrought-iron bar in the corner and began to pour drinks. He was a powerfully built man; his shirt stretched over his back muscles. He had the same thick head of black hair as his son. His legs were very short and rather bandy. He was wearing a white nylon shirt over a string vest, grey trousers, and black lace-up shoes, very shiny, like the type of shoes an off-duty policeman wears. He handed them their drinks. His face showed no trace of the good looks with which his son had been blessed. His skin was swarthy, his mouth thick-lipped, and his eyes were large and pale and slightly protuberant.

Agatha and Roy were seated on a fake leather sofa facing a large desk behind which Terry sat. Zak sat on a hard chair near the door.

'Now, what's all this about us being on telly?' asked Terry.

Agatha, clutching a clipboard, made a speech about covering entertainment in the provinces. Television had become too London-oriented. They needed to find out first some details about the club, the hours it was open, what kind of young people attended, and had they ever had any trouble with the police?

'We had no trouble with the police,' said Terry. 'No drugs here and no under-age drinking, either.' He began to brag about his disco, how he had set it up two years before, after he had moved down from Birmingham when he realized there wasn't much for young people to do in the evenings. Agatha scribbled notes, not caring much what she wrote, as she had no intention of ever using any of it.

At last she said, looking at Zak, 'I was very sad to read about your loss.'

Zak's eyes suddenly filled with tears and he buried his face in his hands. 'We don't want to talk about it,' said Terry gruffly. 'It's a bad business. Now, if you two would like to go down to the club? I'm sure you'll want to talk to some of the young folks.'

Agatha rose, feeling chastened. She had been so sure Zak would turn out to be a villain. She longed to ask him if Kylie had any enemies, but he seemed too genuinely distressed to cope with any questions. Now all she wanted to do was to get out of the club, but she had to pretend to be working for television for a bit longer.

As the noise once more beat upon her ears, she wondered how on earth anyone was supposed to even hear a question. Roy grabbed her and shouted in her ear. 'You go and stand outside and I'll get some of them out there.'

Agatha gratefully made her way outside. She lit a cigarette and waited. Even out on the street, she could feel the beat from the disco reverberating under her feet. She glanced round at the surrounding houses. How could the neighbours stand the noise? Roy then came out, followed by ten excited teenagers, their eyes shining with the prospect of being on television. He and Agatha patiently answered questions of the have-you-met and what-was-he-like variety about pop stars. Roy, because of his high-powered public relations job, knew some of the pop stars they were being questioned about and cheerfully gossiped away. Agatha's head was beginning to itch under the heavy blond wig. She raised her clipboard and asked them for their names and addresses and occupations. Five were unemployed, but one of the girls said she was 'in computers'.

'That wouldn't be the firm where Kylie Stokes worked?' asked Agatha.

'Yes, she worked alongside me at Barrington's,' said the girl.

'And you are?' Agatha squinted down at her clipboard.

'Sharon Heath.'

Sharon was tall and thin. She was wearing a

tube top which exposed a bare midriff. A stud winked in her belly button. She had a stud in her nose and four gold rings in each of her ears. Her make-up was a white mask with eyes ringed in kohl. Although she was young, her shoulders were rounded and everything about her drooped, including her eyes and her thin mouth. Her hair, dyed aubergine, was long and lank.

'It was ever so sad about Kylie,' said Sharon. 'She had the desk next to mine.'

Barrington's, it transpired, was not a computer company, but a firm which supplied bathroom fittings. Sharon worked in what would have been, in the days before computers, the typing pool. Like herself, Kylie had dealt with accounts and orders.

'I gather it's a suspicious death,' said Agatha. 'Did anyone dislike her enough to kill her?'

Sharon put her hand up to her mouth and giggled nervously. 'There's Phyllis.'

Terry Jensen appeared in the doorway. Sharon muttered, 'Got ter go,' and scurried off inside as the rest returned to their questioning of Roy about pop stars.

'We might have got something after all,' said Agatha as they drove out of Evesham. 'I'd like another word with Sharon. I've got her address. I think we should call on her tomorrow.'

'Right,' said Roy. 'You haven't mentioned James.'

'There's nothing *to* mention. Drop the subject.'

As Agatha turned the car into Lilac Lane, she saw lights burning in the author's cottage. She saw the broad, tweedy back of Mrs Anstruther-Jones at the window. She appeared to be talking animatedly.

'My new neighbour's been trapped by the village bore,' commented Agatha.

She parked the car and she and Roy walked indoors.

'You don't seem to have formed a favourable opinion of him,' said Roy.

'I didn't meet him. I saw him, digging the garden.'

'Sure that was him?'

'Why do you ask?'

'Well, when you were describing him, there was a look of amusement in Mrs Bloxby's eyes, as if she were laughing at you.'

Agatha stared at Roy in surprise. 'Mrs Bloxby? You must be joking. Mrs Bloxby would never laugh at me!'

Chapter Three

Sharon Heath lived in a modest terrace house off Port Street, near the income-tax office. The day had turned warm and Agatha's head was once more itching under the blond wig. 'Wait a minute,' said Roy, seizing Agatha's hand as she was just about to ring the bell. 'We haven't decided what we're going to say. We're supposed to be doing research into youth in the provinces in general. Not ask about Kylie in particular.'

'We'll ask the usual boring questions and then just slip it into the conversation,' said Agatha impatiently. Roy gave a resigned shrug. Sometimes, he knew from bitter experience, Agatha had all the tact of a charging rhino.

Agatha rang the bell. They waited quite a few minutes and Agatha was raising her hand to ring the bell again when the door was opened by a blowsy-looking woman wrapped in a dressing-gown. 'Whatever it is, we don't want any.' She made to shut the door.

'We're from television.'

Oh, the magic of television. The woman's hand fluttered up to the rollers in her hair.

'Oh, my! I'm Mrs Heath. Whatever must you think of me? Give me a moment.'

The door slammed.

'What's that all about?' demanded Agatha crossly.

'We're from the telly, so she's gone to pull the rollers out of her hair and cram her nasty, floppy carcass into a body stocking,' said Roy waspishly.

Agatha lit a cigarette. Above, the sky was pale blue, looking as if it had been scrubbed and washed by all the recent rain. The faintest of breezes blew along the street. Church bells clanged out over Evesham. From one of the neighbouring houses a baby set up a crotchety wail.

Finally the door opened and a transformed Mrs Heath stood there, hair lacquered, floury make-up, and figure encased in a tight, imitation-silk dress of imperial purple.

'Come in,' she cooed. 'Sharon was just telling us how you'd been at the club last night. Will my little girl be on the telly?'

'Possibly,' said Agatha briskly. 'She did strike us as being an interesting subject.'

She craned her neck round Agatha. 'Where's the cameraman?'

'That comes later,' said Agatha briskly. 'We have to do the research first.'

'Come in.' Mrs Heath stepped aside. 'The lounge is on your left.'

The lounge was a small room that showed all the signs of having been hurriedly tidied. Agatha sat down on an armchair which crackled because newspapers and magazines had been hurriedly thrust under the seat cushion.

'Now,' said Mrs Heath, 'can I get you some refreshment?' Her mouth was a thin lipsticked line turned down at the corners, and her eyes were hard. Agatha judged that when she was not smarming to visitors, Mrs Heath could very well have a bad temper.

'Nothing for us,' said Agatha. 'Where's Sharon?'

'I'll just get her.'

Mrs Heath sailed from the room. Soon her voice came back to them, harsh and angry. 'For Pete's sake, move your arse, girl. They ain't going to wait all day.'

A few moments later she reappeared, followed by Sharon, who was wearing a blouse of glittery material and a long skirt over a pair of platform-soled boots, the soles so thick they looked like diving boots. She had liberally applied tan make-up which stopped short at her jawline and contrasted sharply with the unhealthy whiteness of her neck.

'Now,' said Agatha, putting her clipboard on her lap. 'We're doing a feature on youth entertainment in the Midlands, but we are also

51

interested in crime. There have been incidents of girls leaving discos late at night and never making it home.'

'I saw about them on the telly, but it ain't happened in Evesham,' said Sharon, picking nervously at her red nail polish.

'There was that Kylie,' broke in Mrs Heath eagerly. ''S in the papers this morning. Says she died of a heroin overdose and the body was frozen first. Did you ever?'

Sharon's plucked eyebrows rose almost to her hairline. 'Drugs! Kylie? Naw.'

'I asked you if she'd had any enemies,' pursued Agatha. 'You said something about someone called Phyllis.'

'I dunno. If this goes on the telly, she'll claw my eyes out.'

'I assure you it won't,' said Agatha. 'I'm just trying to understand how such a thing could have happened.'

'Promise you won't say anythink.'

'Cross our hearts and hope to die,' said Roy solemnly. As if registering his presence for the first time, Sharon gave him a coquettish smile although perhaps 'coquettish' was the wrong way to describe it, thought Agatha. Given that Sharon's mouth was heavily painted with deep-purple lipstick, it had more of a vampire look.

'Well,' said Sharon eagerly and leaning forward to enjoy a now-sanctioned piece of gossip, 'Zak was dating Phyllis. Phyllis is a big girl and ever so noisy when she's had a few. What she didn't know was that Zak was dating Kylie at the same time. One day, Kylie turns up in the office with an engagement ring. Phyllis goes ape-shit and tries to pull Kylie's hair out and we had to separate them. She said, "You'll never marry him. I'll kill you first." There, what do you think of that?'

'Very interesting,' said Agatha. 'Where does this Phyllis live?'

'I can't tell you that,' said Sharon, alarmed. 'She might guess I told you.'

'No reason to,' said Agatha smoothly. 'Is there any way I could interview all the girls she worked with at once?'

'There's McDonald's on the Four Pools. We mostly go there. 'Bout one o'clock.'

'But the police will surely have interviewed Phyllis.'

'They come round to speak to all of us, but we're all so frightened of Phyllis, nobody said a word.'

Feeling that she had got something to go on, Agatha then asked Sharon all about her interests and hobbies – which turned out to be going to the disco and watching soaps on television.

When she had finished, Mrs Heath saw them out, saying, 'You will let us know when the cameras are coming so we can get the place redecorated.'

Agatha, worried at putting the woman to

unnecessary expense, said quickly, 'We'll be doing any filming or interviews at the disco.'

John Armitage shifted restlessly in his chair, vowing to lock the cottage door and never leave it open again. For facing him was Mrs Anstruther-Jones, who had simply walked in without knocking.

She broke off a lecture about her importance in the village as the sound of a car went past the windows of the cottage. 'That'll be your neighbour, Agatha Raisin, and her toy-boy.'

'Really?' he said in a bored voice. 'Now, if you will excuse me –'

'Not that she doesn't occasionally do Good Work.'

'Like underwater basket weaving for the bewildered?'

She stared at him, her mouth open.

'And I really must get on. Got to write.'

She rose and picked up an enormous, shiny leather handbag. 'Ah, your muse,' she said coyly.

'Exactly,' he said, ushering her to the door.

Once she was out, he locked the door behind her. He sat down at his computer and switched it on. He stared at the screen. Agatha Raisin. From village gossip, he gathered she was some sort of amateur detective and had been married to the chap who formerly had this cottage. There was one thing in her favour.

She hadn't come snooping around like almost every other woman in this village. He could only hope that when the novelty of his presence wore off, they would all leave him alone.

Just before noon the following day, he heard the door of his neighbouring cottage slam shut. Suddenly curious to see what this Agatha Raisin looked like, he went to the window on the small landing at the side of his cottage where he could get a view of his neighbour's front door.

A woman was just getting into her car. She had odd-looking blond hair – it looked like a wig – and ugly glasses. 'Well, if that can get herself a toy-boy, good luck to her,' he murmured and went downstairs to start work.

Agatha had run Roy to the London train the evening before, and had to admit she missed his support. She had given him money to buy her a more respectable blond wig, with instructions to post it to her. She could only hope that the excitement of television would stop the young women of Barrington's from questioning her too closely.

Again, the weather was fine. Sun shone in the car windows and the resultant heat made her wig feel even more uncomfortable. She went to Tesco's in Evesham to buy groceries and then arrived at McDonald's at just after one o'clock. Sharon and four other young girls were seated round a table.

Clipboard at the ready, Agatha approached them. 'I think I saw some of you at the disco the other night,' she began. 'I am working on a television programme on the activities of youth in the Midlands. I wonder if I could ask you a few questions?'

They eagerly made room for her. She took down their names as an opening gambit. As well as Sharon, the others were Ann Trump, Mary Webster, Joanna Field, and Phyllis Heger. They said only one, Marilyn Josh, was missing. She had a hair appointment. Agatha studied Phyllis. Everything about her was large, although she was not fat. It all looked like solid muscle. She had large brown eyes, a large full-lipped mouth, thick black hair, and a generous bust. Her eyes glared this way and that, as if she were in a perpetual temper.

Agatha proceeded to ask them the same general questions she had asked Sharon, and noticed that Phyllis mostly butted in with all the answers. They resented Phyllis's hogging the limelight, Agatha could see that. When she herself had been working her way up, starting with lowly office jobs, Agatha had been amazed to find that each office seemed to contain one bully. She longed to put Phyllis down, but at the moment she was a suspect and Agatha didn't want to alienate her. She decided not to ask any questions about Kylie, but to try to arrange a meeting with Phyllis and get the girl on her own.

So Agatha wrote and wrote and then said brightly, 'You will get tired of all my questions, but this is simply the start. We do an awful lot of research before we actually start filming.'

They all said eagerly it was no trouble at all.

Agatha thanked them and went to her car.

She was about to get in when she heard the rapid clack of high heels behind her. She turned round and found herself confronted by Phyllis. 'You should really talk to me,' said Phyllis. 'I've got more sophistication than what them have.'

'What if I meet you after work?' suggested Agatha.

'That would be ever so nice,' said Phyllis in a sort of strangulated voice she seemed to imagine was upper-class. 'Where?'

'There's a pub called The Grapes in Evesham High Street. Know it?'

'Yes, but no one much goes there.'

'I know,' said Agatha. 'It's a good place for a quiet chat. I'll see you there at, say, six o'clock.'

'Right you are,' said Phyllis, those large eyes alight with a sort of ferocious vanity.

John Armitage was heading up the stairs of his cottage when he heard a car drive up to his neighbour's cottage. Once more he looked out of the landing window. Yes, it was that Raisin female, all right. Then he stared. For Agatha Raisin jerked the blond wig off her head and threw it on the car seat and then took off her glasses. Had she been in disguise? Or did she really think, perhaps, that she looked younger in that dreadful wig? A pair of good legs emerged from the driving seat as she opened the car door. The sun shone down on her glossy brown hair cut in a fashionable style.

Curiouser and curiouser, thought John. I might just call on her.

Agatha fed her cats. She was sure she had already fed them, but they looked hungry. She had cooked them fresh fish. She herself ate microwaved meals, but she went to a lot of trouble to see her cats had the best. She bent down and stroked their warm furry heads, feeling a wave of loneliness engulf her. Her cats, Hodge and Boswell, never really seemed to need her except as a source of food. She glanced at the kitchen clock. Time to get ready to meet the dreadful Phyllis. She remembered she had left her wig in the car along with her glasses and went out to fetch them.

Returning, she went upstairs to the bathroom and made up her face and put the wig and glasses back on. She wondered briefly why no one had called around to ask her why she was always going out in disguise. There was a ring at the doorbell.

Agatha went down and opened the door. A tall, good-looking man stood there. He had a lightly tanned face, green eyes and a strong chin. But he was carrying a Bible.

'No!' said Agatha, and slammed the door in his face.

Mormons, she thought, as she picked up her handbag. They always send the best-looking ones around.

John Armitage retreated to his cottage. He had found the Bible in a cupboard with James Lacey's name on it and thought if he took it along next door it would be a good excuse to meet his neighbour.

Well, at least he now knew there was one woman in the village who most definitely did not want to have anything to do with him. He went upstairs to pack. He planned to spend a few days in London visiting an old friend.

Agatha opened the door to the musty interior of The Grapes. It had neither piped music nor one-armed bandits nor pool table and so was shunned by the youth of Evesham. Phyllis was already there, drinkless.

'May I get you something?'

'A dry martini,' said Phyllis, who normally drank vodka and Red Bull, but thought a dry martini sounded sophisticated.

'I don't think that's a good idea,' said Agatha. 'They probably don't know how to make one. What about a gin and tonic? That's what I'm having.'

'All right, then,' said Phyllis ungraciously. 'Make it a large one.'

Agatha came back to the table carrying two large gin and tonics. 'Perhaps instead of asking you questions, you begin by telling me about your life,' said Agatha. 'I'm surprised a pretty girl like you isn't engaged.'

'I'm hard to please,' replied Phyllis. 'I think someone like me should move to London. I'm wasted down here. Nothing ever happens here.'

'I wouldn't say that,' said Agatha. 'Floods. Murder.'

'Murder?'

'Kylie Stokes.'

'Oh, her. Load of rubbish, that. Take it from me. It was suicide.'

'How come?'

'Can I have another?' Phyllis had managed to gulp down her gin and tonic.

Agatha went back to the bar and returned with two more drinks.

'You were saying . . .?'

'Oh, about Kylie? If you ask me, that wedding would never have taken place.'

'Why? I mean, she had the wedding gown and everything.'

'Zak proposed to her on the rebound.'

'From whom?'

'From me.'

'So you had dumped him?'

'We had this row. We were always having rows. We were hot in bed. Let me tell you . . .'

Phyllis proceeded to give a description of her sexual prowess in anatomical detail.

Amazing, thought Agatha. It was all the fault of those women's magazines which led young girls to believe that the only way to keep a man was to indulge in the tricks of the brothel. But, then, maybe she was being old-fashioned. The very word modesty, as applied to women, had gone out of fashion a long time ago. She averted her eyes from Phyllis's thick red lips, trying to fight down a feeling of revulsion at what those lips had done, and said, 'The body was frozen. You don't commit suicide and then freeze yourself.'

'Police have got it wrong,' remarked Phyllis.

'Did you know she was on heroin?'

'Oh, sure.'

'No track marks.'

'She probably sniffed the stuff.'

'And were you very upset when Zak became engaged to Kylie?'

'I s'pose you'll hear it from the other girls. I was furious. He was only getting rnarried to her to spite me.'

'But there was some sort of hen party for her, was there not? Did you go to that?'

'Naw. Silly business. Then Kylie disappeared the day afterwards. The Stokes family had the police round at the office questioning us all. But the police seemed to think she'd had wedding nerves and had done a runner.'

'And what did you think?'

'I told Zak she'd only wanted a ring to show off to the other girls, but she didn't care for him.'

'So you saw Zak? When was this?'

''Bout a day before she was found. He came round my house that evening.'

'And was he upset?'

Phyllis gave a coarse laugh. 'Not after I'd seen to him, he wasn't.'

'You mean you had sex?'

'What d'you think?'

Agatha had a memory of Zak weeping at the club. She thought Phyllis was one horrible out-and-out liar.

'What's all this about Kylie?' asked Phyllis suspiciously. 'I thought we were here to talk about me.'

'And so we are,' said Agatha evenly. 'Don't you realize that to have known someone who was mysteriously murdered makes you newsworthy?'

'It was suicide,' said Phyllis mulishly. 'Now let's talk about me.'

She proceeded to brag. She had always

fancied herself on television, she said, because she had a good personality and was a looker.

I hate you, thought Agatha as Phyllis bragged on. I bet you're capable of murder. I bet you're a narcissist, and a psychotic one at that. All the while, she pretended to take notes.

'And you live alone?' she asked when Phyllis finally paused for breath. 'Let me see, 10A Jones Terrace, is that right? Where is your family?'

'Over in Worcester.'

I wish I were a policeman and I could ask her where she was on the days before the murder, thought Agatha. I must phone Bill and see if they know exactly when she was murdered. I must see Kylie's mother. When exactly did she go missing? Did she return after the hen party? But she must have gone home to get the wedding dress. And why would she put it on and leave the house dressed in it? To show someone? To show Zak? If only she had not adopted this stupid television role, she could revert to herself and ask questions until Zak and his father threw her out, but at least it would be more straightforward. She missed James. Even Charles would have done. She needed someone as back-up. Of course, she could always go and see Worcester police, but she was well aware that they considered her an interfering busybody.

Phyllis's voice was churning on, about how her family didn't appreciate her ambitions and that was why she had left home. They had been dragging her down. I'll talk to the others apart from Sharon and Phyllis separately, thought Agatha, and set her clipboard down on the table and said resolutely, 'I think that's more than enough for now.'

Phyllis looked disappointed, but Agatha said she had other people to interview. She took a note of Phyllis's home phone number and with relief escaped out into the evening air of Evesham. She glanced at her watch. Only six-thirty. Agatha felt that Phyllis had been talking for hours. She hurried off. Phyllis had gone to the loo in the pub but might appear at any minute and start talking again.

She walked off rapidly along the High Street in the direction of Merstow Green where she had left her car. She was passing a bookshop when she suddenly stopped and stared in the window, which was still lit. The shop sold remaindered books, but the bookseller often had a few titles by popular authors at knock-down prices. There was a display of one of John Armitage's books, not the one Agatha had read, and one of them was turned round to show the picture of the author on the back.

Agatha found herself looking down at the face of the man she had mistaken for a Mormon. The man she had seen digging the garden must have been a gardener he had hired. Damn Mrs Bloxby for a devious woman. That's why she had looked amused when she,

Agatha, had described the gardener instead of the author. Well, it all went to show what a rotten influence the church was on people.

Agatha forgot her burst of temper as she drove homewards. John Armitage was certainly attractive. She would call on him and apologize and they would both laugh over her mistake ... and ... and ...

Wrapped in rosy dreams, Agatha dashed into her cottage, removed the wig and glasses, changed into a clinging red dress and high heels, after putting on fresh make-up, and rushed next door. No one. The cottage stood dark and silent. And his car wasn't parked outside.

The next day Agatha received a visit from Detective Inspector John Brudge of the Worcester police. 'Come in,' said Agatha, delighted. She thought he had called to enlist her help, for had she not solved an Evesham murder before? He was accompanied by a detective sergeant and a detective constable.

'Mrs Raisin,' said Brudge severely, 'we are questioning everyone connected with the death of Kylie Stokes.'

'Yes,' said Agatha eagerly. 'I know a bit about –'

He cut across her. 'And it has come to our ears that some woman, saying she is arranging a television programme, has been asking questions. We have checked with all the television companies and not one of them knows of this woman.'

Agatha's heart sank.

'What's her name?' she asked feebly.

'That is what's so amazing. She didn't give one. Everyone is so gullible when it comes to thinking they are dealing with someone who claims to represent a television company. This woman was described as middle-aged, blond and with glasses. Now, we haven't got a search warrant but we can get one today to find if you have a blond wig and glasses in this house. Do you want to tell us the truth, or do I have to get that warrant?'

Agatha bit her lip. Then she gave a shrug. 'Yes, that was me.'

'Before I consider charging you with obstructing police business, tell me what you have learned.'

Too worried to hold anything back, Agatha told them what she had found out, about Zak's distress, about Phyllis's story, about the other girls.

Brudge listened to her impassively and then said, 'Would you mind waiting in the other room?'

He saw her across the hall and into the kitchen and then shut the door behind her.

'What do you think?' Brudge asked his detective sergeant, a young man called Norris.

'Interfering busybody,' said Norris. 'I'd book her, sir, and get her out of our hair.'

'That's what I should do. On the other hand, she's capable of digging up stuff the people concerned wouldn't tell a policeman.'

'But, sir, we're dealing with a murder investigation. She could get killed.'

'Yes, she could, couldn't she? I'll give her a rap on the knuckles but I won't stop her.'

He went and jerked open the door, fully expecting to find Agatha listening outside, but he found she was still in the kitchen. She was sitting on the floor, playing with her cats.

'I must give you a severe warning, Mrs Raisin, about the penalties of interfering in a police investigation. But as a favour to you for having been of some little, very little, assistance to us in the past, we will not tell those you have interviewed your real identity. That will be all. Oh, one other thing. Anything else you do find out, you are to report to me immediately. Here is my card. It has my office number, home number and mobile phone number.'

'Thank you,' said Agatha meekly.

After they had left, Agatha turned over what he had said and then her face cleared. They weren't going to stop her.

Agatha was admiring a splendid blond wig which had arrived by special delivery from

Roy when the doorbell rang again. She found a woman she did not know standing on the step.

'Mrs Raisin,' she said. 'I am Freda Stokes, Kylie's mother.'

'Come in,' said Agatha. 'Come through to the kitchen. Would you like a cup of tea? I am very sorry about your sad loss.'

Freda Stokes was a sturdy woman with round apple cheeks with a high colour. Her grizzled hair was frizzy and her hands rough and red. She had large eyes of an indeterminate colour.

She refused the offer of tea and settled her battered handbag firmly on her capacious lap and studied Agatha. 'I've heard you're a sort of detective.'

'In a way,' said Agatha.

'I'll pay you to find out who killed my daughter. Won't be much. I've a stall at the market. Glass animals. Don't make much.'

'I'll do it for nothing,' said Agatha.

'I won't take charity.'

'I'm fairly well off and you aren't,' said Agatha bluntly. 'I'll do it. Wait till I get some paper. I'll need to ask you questions. Do you feel up to it?'

'I'm up to anything,' said Freda grimly, 'if it'll nail the bastard who killed my daughter.'

Agatha darted through to her desk and returned with a sheaf of papers.

'So tell me when you last saw her?'

'It was two days before she died. She'd been to some sort of hen party with the girls in her office. She was a bit tiddly when she came home, that would be around midnight. I told her to get straight to bed. She said she'd had a good time. She said that girl, Phyllis Heger, who was always picking on her, wasn't there. As she was off work, I thought I'd let her have a long lie-in. My husband's dead. There was only me and Kylie.' A fat tear slid down her cheek. Agatha handed her a box of tissues and waited until she had composed herself.

'I went to the market early as usual. I came back at dinnertime.' Agatha knew she meant lunchtime. They still had dinner in the middle of the day in Evesham. 'The house was quiet. Lazy girl, I thought, and went to wake her. Her bed was empty. Hadn't been slept in. I called Zak, I called her work, I called her friends, then I called the police. They didn't take it seriously. They said brides always got nervous before a wedding and she'd turn up. Then I found her wedding dress was missing. I phoned them again. But again they wouldn't take me seriously. That was until she turned up dead.'

'What about Zak?' asked Agatha. 'Could he possibly have done it?'

'No, he adored her, and he and his father have been marvellous to me. I couldn't have got through the last few days without them. Zak's broken up.'

'And you never had any suspicion that Kylie might be on drugs?'

'My Kylie? Never! She was part of a youth group at the church. They're very down on drugs.'

'So why do you think she took her wedding dress?'

'Like I said, she'd had a bit to drink. I think one of them girls said she wanted to see the dress. Kylie was ever so proud of it. I think she took it round to one of their houses. She might have been attacked on the road home. It's hard to get a cab.'

'She'd change back into her ordinary clothes, surely,' said Agatha. 'And whoever she had been visiting, if they had nothing to hide, then why wouldn't they come forward?'

'Maybe whoever it was might be frightened of being suspected.'

'What about Phyllis Heger?'

'She wasn't at the office party, like I said.'

'I don't know if you know this, Mrs Stokes –'

'Freda.'

'Right, then, Freda. I don't know if you know that Zak, according to Phyllis, was dating her.'

'Oh, Kylie told me about that. She said Phyllis hated her. Do you think it could have been her?'

'I'd like to think so,' said Agatha. 'I don't like her. But just think of the organization! Could Phyllis have injected her with heroin and then

70

dumped her body in a freezer chest, and then somehow got it into the river? Was Kylie dating anyone before Zak?'

'She was engaged once before, to Harry McCoy.'

'Who's he?'

'He's a machine-tool operator at Barrington's. Steady chap. I liked him.'

'What's his address?'

Freda gave it to her and Agatha wrote it down.

Agatha leaned forward. 'I'd better tell you something in confidence. I've already been investigating your daughter's murder. I've been going around masquerading as someone from television, wearing a disguise of blond wig and glasses. If you hear about such a person, you'll know it's me.' Agatha thought about Brudge. Had he really been encouraging her to go ahead?

'Worcester police are very good,' she said cautiously. 'They'll probably get to the bottom of it eventually. What about drugs? I didn't think they'd be that much of a problem in a quiet place like Evesham. You work at the market. You must hear things.'

'Evesham's like everywhere else, riddled with the stuff,' said Freda bitterly. 'They found a pub dealing in drugs and closed it down. Nobody knows where it's all coming from now.'

'The people who take drugs must know,' said Agatha. 'Ever hear of anything connected to the club?'

'Not even one Ecstasy tablet. It's been raided at least once. A few under-age drinkers, that's all.'

'Give me your phone number,' said Agatha. 'I'll let you know anything I find out.'

'Bless you,' said Freda, tears now coursing freely down her cheeks. 'I've been feeling so helpless.'

Agatha handed her a wad of tissues. When Freda had recovered, Agatha saw her out and then returned to the kitchen and sat down, feeling guilty. After all, she did not deserve Freda's blessing for pursuing an investigation out of no higher motive than curiosity and a desire to allay the boredom of retirement in a country village. Mrs Bloxby was the one with pure motives. Or was she?

By omission, she had deliberately led Agatha to believe the new neighbour wasn't worth bothering about. She had some explaining to do.

Some ten minutes later, Mrs Bloxby found herself facing a truculent Agatha in the vicarage drawing-room.

'I shouldn't try to manipulate your life,' said Mrs Bloxby ruefully. 'But I did not want to see you fall enamoured of another neighbour and get hurt.'

'Do you know what I did?' demanded Agatha wrathfully. 'He came to my door carrying a Bible, and I thought he was a Mormon and slammed the door in his face.'

Mrs Bloxby snorted with laughter.

'It's not funny!' howled Agatha. 'What was he carrying a Bible for anyway?'

'He left it with me,' said Mrs Bloxby when she had stopped laughing. 'It was James's Bible. He found it in a closet. I'll get it for you.'

She went out and then returned carrying the Bible. Agatha opened it and noticed James's name written in his familiar handwriting inside. A wave of love and loss engulfed her and she clutched the Bible and stared at Mrs Bloxby with miserable eyes.

'It'll pass,' said Mrs Bloxby. 'All things pass.'

Agatha firmly put the Bible away from her. 'So tell me about John Armitage.'

'I know very little. Just that he's a successful writer. He seems very pleasant. I gather he was once married and is divorced. I think the Anstruther-Jones woman has been bothering him. I told him not to answer the door to her and she would soon get tired of calling on him.' Mrs Bloxby looked at Agatha ruefully. 'I'm afraid I told him not to answer the door to any of the women. They have all been pestering him, taking him cakes and home-made jam or copies of his books for him to autograph.'

So I can't do any of those things, thought Agatha. Rats.

'I wish you had told me the truth,' she said severely. 'I am not a child.'

'No, I shouldn't have misled you, but the temptation was irresistible. I won't do it again.'

'Sometimes I wonder about you,' said Agatha. 'Anyway, that dead girl's mother has just called on me. She wants me to investigate her daughter's death. She even offered to pay me.'

'It must have made you feel like a real detective.'

'I am a real detective,' snapped Agatha, who had not quite forgiven the vicar's wife for misleading her about John Armitage.

'Of course. How are you getting on?'

Agatha outlined her findings. Mrs Bloxby listened carefully. Then she said, 'Someone's dealing drugs in Evesham. Could it be possible that Kylie stumbled across the source?'

'Then that would suggest the club.'

'Not necessarily. One of those girls could have said something, let something slip. They must all have had a bit too much to drink at that hen party. Maybe one of them panicked and told her supplier.'

'Far-fetched,' said Agatha grumpily because she had not considered such a possibility herself.

'Possibly. Would you like some tea?'

'No, thank you.'

'You'll need to forgive me sometime.'

'I have forgiven you,' lied Agatha and stumped out.

When she got home, she went over her notes and then logged everything she had in the computer. Whom should she approach that evening? Perhaps she should start with Harry McCoy before going on to one of the other girls. She looked at her watch and remembered she had a Pilates class and rushed to change into tights and a T-shirt before driving fast to Evesham. By the time she returned home, she was feeling relaxed and refreshed. Still no sign of John Armitage in residence, she noted.

Later that day, she put on the new blond wig, tying it in a neat pony-tail. It looked much more natural than the old one, and the spectacles with the plain glass lenses really did make her look different. She hesitated before leaving. Was the disguise really necessary? Mrs Stokes had asked her to investigate, so she could surely go as herself. But, then, Harry McCoy might be friendly with the girls. He might even be the villain!

So Agatha set off, feeling very lonely. She missed Roy's chattering company. When she parked in Merstow Green, she took out a street map of Evesham and checked on Harry McCoy's address. He lived not far from the car park in Horres Street. She decided to walk. The streets away from the High Street seemed strangely deserted. No children played outside. Televisions flickered behind lace-curtained windows. The wind had risen, and fallen cherry blossoms swirled in front of Agatha. It had turned unseasonably cold. She located the small red-brick terraced house in which he lived. It looked dark and empty. There were two bells, one for upstairs and one for downstairs, but no one answered the summons of either.

Agatha retreated. She decided to go back to the car park and then call back at the house from time to time. She had forgotten her clipboard with the addresses of the other girls and was reluctant to go all the way home to get it. She sat in her car, smoking and listening to the radio, venturing out once more to take the long walk back to Harry's house. She wished she had decided to park outside, but there was not a single parking space left in the street and to double-park would draw unwelcome attention to herself.

By ten o'clock, she got wearily out of her car again. Just one more time. To her relief, there was a light shining in the upstairs window. She pressed the bell and waited.

No reply.

She pressed it again and stepped back and looked up. No curtain twitched. No face looked down at her. Should she try the neighbours? No, scrub that. She didn't want him to know she was looking for him or to start lying to neighbours about some fictitious television programme.

Agatha wearily turned away. A wasted evening. Why not just forget the whole thing and leave it to the police? She began to walk slowly along the deserted street.

And then she sensed danger.

Afterwards, she could not say why or what had alerted her or where the sudden feeling of menace had come from. She heard a car approaching. She twisted her head, saw head-lights blazing, and in one split second realized the car was rushing at her at full speed.

She threw herself over the garden hedge next to her, hearing the car roar past as it mounted the pavement where she had been standing and then hearing it lurch back on to the road. She lay in someone's front garden, shivering and panting. A door opened.

The next thing she knew was that someone was standing over her. She straightened up, ridiculously relieved to find that her wig was still in place.

'What the 'ell do you think you're doing?' demanded a small, thin woman angrily.

Agatha struggled up. 'I'm sorry. I must have had a fainting fit and fallen over your hedge.'

She swayed and then regained her balance. Despite her shock and fright, she did not want to say she had been nearly killed. Questions would be asked. The police called. And this time Brudge would really tell her to leave the whole thing alone.

'I know your sort,' said the woman wrathfully. 'Drunk, that's what you are. And at your age. You oughter be ashamed of yourself.'

Agatha made for the garden gate. One of her high-heeled shoes got caught in a loose brick on the path and she stumbled and nearly fell. 'Get out o' here,' shouted the woman. 'And sober up!'

Agatha felt that the walk to her car was the longest she had ever taken. She did not even feel safe when she was in her car. She accelerated out of the car park at speed.

John Armitage had cut short his stay in London and was making his way leisurely down the road into Carsely when a car he recognized as his neighbour's shot past him and hurtled off in front of him. 'Crazy driver,' he muttered.

He proceeded at a reasonable rate and then parked in front of his cottage. Before he switched off his headlights, he saw his neighbour's car and that she was still in it, hunched over the wheel.

He was about to open the gate and go in when he hesitated. Maybe she was ill.

John approached Agatha's car cautiously and then looked in the window. She had her face in her hands and her shoulders were heaving. He rapped on the glass.

Agatha straightened up and gave him a look of wild terror.

He opened the car door. 'I'm John Armitage. Your neighbour. We haven't really met. Is there anything I can do?'

Agatha took a tissue out of a box on the seat beside her and blew her nose. 'I had a fright,' she blurted out. 'They tried to kill me.'

'Was it road rage? I'll call the police for you.'

Agatha shook her head. She had been crying because, unnerved as she was, she had been feeling terribly alone. No Charles or James or even Roy to comfort her.

'Would you like a brandy or something?'

Agatha gave a choked sob. Then she said, 'Help me indoors and I'll tell you about it.'

Chapter Four

Once indoors, Agatha settled John in the living room with a drink and went upstairs. She removed the wig and glasses and put on fresh make-up, reflecting that the best treatment for shock must surely be the company of a good-looking man.

John looked up as she entered. She certainly had made a remarkable recovery, he thought.

Agatha poured herself a shot of brandy and sat down opposite him.

'Thank you for your help,' she said. 'I don't want the police to know about this. You see, someone's just tried to kill me.'

He did not exclaim or protest that she should indeed tell the police, but merely looked at her questioningly.

She began to tell him all about the death of Kylie and about how she was masquerading as a television producer. John Armitage smiled.

'What's so funny?' demanded Agatha.

'It explains the blond wig. You should really

take it off before you return to Carsely. Your disguise has caused a lot of speculation. Mrs Anstruther-Jones thinks she has the answer.'

'What's that?'

'That you have a toy-boy and are striving to look younger.'

Agatha's face flamed with anger. 'Silly old bat.'

'Go on. You were telling me about this mystery.'

So Agatha proceeded to tell him the rest of it, ending up by saying that she did not want to report the attempt on her life because the police would be furious with her.

'So what are you going to do now?'

'Go on. If I got attacked just because I was trying to see Harry McCoy, then he might be the clue I need.'

He looked at her thoughtfully and then he said, 'You've done this sort of thing before?'

'Yes,' said Agatha. She was about to brag about other cases, but her knees began to shake. She was still not over her shock. Had she shown off in her usual way, then John Armitage would have lost interest in her. But the very fact that she was not flirting or simpering or trying to impress him endeared her to him.

'You show a great deal of courage,' he said. 'Were you always on your own when things like this happened before?'

'I usually had someone helping me. My ex-husband, James, or a friend, Charles. But I'm on my own in this one. I must admit I had a bad fright. I might leave it for a few days.'

He looked at the clock. 'Goodness. It's one in the morning. I'd better let you get some sleep.'

And that's that, thought Agatha. She racked her brains trying to think of a way to keep him or suggest another meeting, but she was too shaky and tired.

He rose to his feet. 'I tell you what: why don't you leave everything to Sunday, and I'll come with you and we'll talk to this McCoy fellow on Sunday morning, when he's off work.'

'Thank you,' said Agatha. 'What time?'

'I'll pick you up at nine in the morning.'

Then Agatha's face fell. 'Your face is on the jacket of one of your books in Evesham. You'll be recognized. I didn't know what you looked like until I saw your photo. You see, when you arrived on my doorstep, carrying that Bible, I thought you were a Mormon.'

He laughed. 'What have you got against the Mormons?'

'Nothing at all. I'm sure they are splendid people. I just don't like being preached at on my own doorstep.'

'I have no intention of going in disguise,' he said. 'You can say you have drafted in a celebrity author to help you with the script. I have done television scripts before.'

'Then I'll see you Sunday.'

After he had gone, Agatha went upstairs, undressed, washed, put on a voluminous night-gown and crawled under the duvet. The events of the evening now seemed like a dream. He was a handsome man. How old was he? Despite his looks, probably around fifty. But men who kept their looks and figures after the age of forty were usually gay. Still, she found the thought of his support comforting. And, she told herself firmly, she had no intention of starting to think romantically about him.

She fell asleep and woke two hours later, suddenly sweating with fear. The old cottage creaked and the wind sighed around outside. Agatha switched on the bedside light and then got out and switched on the overhead light as well. Her cats, who usually slept downstairs in their basket, appeared in the bedroom at that moment and climbed on to the bed. She settled down with a cat on either side of her and their purring soon soothed her back to sleep.

'How old do you think John Armitage is?' Agatha asked Mrs Bloxby when the vicar's wife called on her the next day.

'Older than he looks. Miss Simms said she read an article about him. He's actually fifty-three.'

'I think he's gay,' said Agatha.

'Despite the fact that he's been married? Why?'

'Heterosexual men let themselves go.'

'Not necessarily. Look at my husband. Alf's in good shape.'

Agatha thought of the vicar – grey-haired, glasses, scholarly, slightly stooped – and reflected that love was indeed blind.

'But to get back to the attempt on your life,' said Mrs Bloxby. 'That really worries me. Couldn't you even tell Bill Wong about it?'

'Bill Wong is a dear friend, but he's a policeman, first and last. He would feel obliged to put in a report.'

'Anything to do with drugs is highly dangerous,' cautioned Mrs Bloxby.

'I can't understand it,' said Agatha, half joking. 'I thought all the drug barons had gone over to smuggling cigarettes. They keep jacking up the price so it's getting a bit like the States during prohibition. Do you know, there was an item on the news that said that twenty-five per cent of the British population bought their cigarettes on the black market. No one's ever approached me.'

'I think you're in enough trouble as it is without buying contraband cigarettes,' said Mrs Bloxby severely. 'Anyway, I thought you were giving them up.'

'I will, I will.' Agatha lit a cigarette. 'When this case is over.'

'If you're still alive. Why don't you believe Phyllis's story that she and Zak had sex?'

'Because she's a nasty bitch and a compulsive liar.'

'Still ... Let's think about Zak. It appears Kylie was a decent girl and her mother is a sterling woman. What sort of man orders his fiancée to get a bikini wax before the wedding? I mean, a lot of women who are going on their honeymoon get it done as a matter of course, not because of sex, but because of those thong swimsuits or even the ones that are high-cut on the leg.'

'How do you know all this?'

'I'm not totally cut off from the world.'

'But Zak was genuinely upset about her death. Those weren't fake tears.'

'Keep an open mind and do be careful, dear Mrs Raisin.'

'I'll have John to look after me.'

'May I give you some advice?'

'I hate it when people say that. Okay, go on.'

'I think it's important you have some sort of protection during your inquiries,' said Mrs Bloxby. 'But men do not like *needy* women. Believe me, they can smell needy across two continents. Please do not think of him in terms of romance. I think he could be easily driven away.'

'I don't fancy him,' said Agatha sulkily. 'You seem to think I'm like some sort of teenager.'

That was what the vicar's wife did think but she refrained from saying so.

Half an hour after Mrs Bloxby had left, the doorbell went again. Agatha gave a nervous shiver but reassured herself that the sun was shining brightly outside, and the villain or villains, whoever they were, surely did not know her real identity. Unless they followed you home, came the heart-stopping thought. She peered through the spyhole she'd had installed in the door. At first she did not recognize the man standing outside, and then, with surprise, she did. She opened the door.

'Charles?'

It was indeed Sir Charles Fraith, her old friend and sometime lover. But instead of being small, and neat and slim, he was decidedly chubby. His hair had thinned and he had a double chin.

'Come in,' said Agatha. 'I've a pot of coffee in the kitchen. Although I shouldn't even be speaking to you. Why didn't you invite me to your wedding? I could have flown over to Paris.'

Charles sat down at the kitchen table. 'I couldn't. You see, I'd told my wife, Anne-Marie, that we'd once been . . . er . . . intimate. It came up, sort of, when I was telling her about some of the murder cases we'd been involved in. She ordered me not to invite you.'

'So what does she think about you being here today?'

'She doesn't know. I don't like to upset her. She's expecting twins.'

Agatha put a mug of coffee down in front of him. 'So what did you come for?' she demanded harshly.

'Curious to see how you were getting along.'

'Splendidly, thank you.'

'Any news of James?'

'No.'

'Any murders? What about this business in Evesham?'

'Nothing to do with me,' lied Agatha. 'Look, Charles, I wish you would just finish your coffee and go. I'm sore because you didn't invite me to the wedding. Even though you had blabbed to your bride about me, you could have insisted, or at least have had the guts to phone me up and tell me about it.'

'I told you. I let slip about us to Anne-Marie and so she wouldn't let me invite you. I didn't want to rock the boat. I don't want to have a failed marriage like yours, Aggie. Marriage takes work,' he said pompously.

Agatha leaned across the table and slid his coffee mug away from him. 'Get out, Charles. I'd forgotten how insensitive you can be.'

'What about a kiss for old times' sake?'

'OUT!!!'

'No need to get sore. I'm going.'

He walked off stiffly, giving Agatha a good view of his now large bottom.

Agatha ran to the door and shouted just as Charles was getting into his car, 'And don't come back!'

Agatha then saw John Armitage, who was entering his front door with a bag of groceries, staring at her and gave him a weak smile before retreating indoors.

'I hate it when people change,' grumbled Agatha to her cats. Charles had really only changed in appearance, but to admit that to herself would have made Agatha feel worse.

On Sunday, Agatha's alarm failed to work and she awoke to find it was a quarter to nine, so instead of the long session she had planned with make-up and clothes, she washed quickly and dressed in the first clothes that came to hand, and put on a little foundation cream and lipstick before scrambling down the stairs just as the doorbell rang.

'Ready?' asked John. He was wearing a blue shirt under a soft suede jacket and casual trousers.

'Ready,' said Agatha breathlessly.

'No disguise?'

'Rats! Won't be a minute.' Agatha ran back up the stairs and put on the blond wig and glasses.

'I meant to advise you to put on your disguise in the car,' said John when she reappeared. 'No, leave it now,' he added as Agatha reached up a hand to pull the wig off again. 'We'll take my car.'

He drove out of the village, smoothly and competently, while Agatha tried to think of things to say but felt unusually shy. At last she said, 'I hope he's at home.'

'We'll try anyway. How are you feeling?'

'I'm all right now. Things are never so scary in daylight.'

'I've never done anything like this before,' said John. 'In fact, I've never lived in a village before. Always been in cities.'

'Like Birmingham? I read one of your books and it was based in Birmingham.'

'I only did research there. No, I lived in London until my divorce.'

'And when was that?'

'Two years ago.'

'An amicable divorce?'

'Had to be done without fuss on her part. She had been unfaithful to me too many times.'

'Did that hurt?' asked Agatha curiously.

'Not now. I'm glad it's all over. What about you?'

'He left me for the church. Last I heard, he's in some monastery in France.'

'That must have been difficult.'

Agatha sighed. 'I never really had him. It

was an odd marriage. We were like two bachelors rather than a married couple.'

'That wasn't the man I heard you shouting at a few days ago?'

'No, that was someone else. I don't want to talk about it.'

'Okay.'

'Why do you set your stories in inner cities?' asked Agatha. 'You don't look like an inner-city person.'

He had a pleasant, cultured voice, no trace of accent.

'I wanted to write about real people.'

'Sordid surroundings don't make people real,' said Agatha with sudden passion as she remembered her own impoverished upbringing. 'Their minds are often twisted with drink or drugs and their bodies old before their time with cheap junk food.'

'You sound as if you are speaking from personal experience.'

Agatha was a snob, and Agatha was not going to admit she had been brought up in a Birmingham slum. 'I'm a good observer,' she said quickly.

'I thought I was, too. We must talk some more about this.'

When they got to Evesham, Agatha instructed him to park in Merstow Green. They left the car and were soon walking down the road that Agatha had so recently fled along in terror. People were ambling about, women pushing babies in prams, men talking in groups; it all looked so harmless.

They arrived at the house. 'Which bell?' he asked. 'There aren't any names.'

'The light was on in the upstairs before I was attacked.'

'We'll try that.'

He rang the bell.

They waited a few minutes. Then John said, 'May as well try the bottom one,' and rang it.

The door was opened by a young man, a very clean young man. He had neat light brown hair, a round face, a gleaming white short-sleeved shirt and jeans with creases like knife-edges. 'Mr McCoy?' asked Agatha.

'Yes, but if you're selling anything –'

'No, we represent a television company. We can't cover the young people of Evesham without mentioning Kylie's death. We would, of course, like to know what sort of amusements young people enjoy in a town like this. May we come in?'

'I've got someone with me at the moment,' he said. 'Can we go somewhere? There's a café along towards the river.'

'That'll do fine.'

'I'll get my jacket.'

He closed the door. 'Seems a nice enough fellow,' said John.

'Shhh!' said Agatha.

'Why can't I come, too?' demanded a shrill female voice. Harry McCoy mumbled something in return and then the door opened. His face was red with embarrassment.

They walked along the road together until they came to a café, the kind that sold light snacks. They took a table at the window. Outside, the river Avon slid along on its green-black way. A launch cruised past, sending waves of water to either bank.

'I'm surprised this place is still open,' said Agatha. 'I thought it would have been flooded out.'

'It came right up to the doors,' said Harry. 'Mrs Joyce, that's her behind the counter, who owns the place, had piles of sandbags at the front. Also the café's higher up on a sort of mound than the houses on either side. They got the worst of it.'

John returned from the counter, where he had gone to fetch cups of coffee.

Agatha started by asking him questions about how young people amused themselves. Harry said sometimes they went up to Birmingham, a few of them sharing a car and taking turns at staying sober.

'And what about Hollywood Nights, the disco?'

'I wouldn't be seen dead there,' said Harry. 'Lot of layabouts.'

'You were engaged to Kylie?'

'Yes.'

'What went wrong with the engagement?'

'Zak's what went wrong,' said Harry moodily. 'Have you seen that car of his?'

Agatha shook her head.

'It's a Jag. It turned her head. He took to waiting outside Barrington's for her when she finished work and offering her a lift home. Phyllis Heger, she was engaged to Zak at the time, had told him Kylie was a virgin, and he said something like he would soon see to that. I tried to warn her. I couldn't believe it when she broke off her engagement to me and became engaged to him.'

'I thought Phyllis would be here any moment,' said Agatha.

'Why?'

'That was her with you this morning. I recognized her voice.'

'I told her we were going to Butler's in the High Street,' said Harry and flushed under Agatha's curious gaze.

'And are you and Phyllis an item?'

He flushed again. 'Naw. Phyllis is ... Well, she's just a girl. Not the kind you get serious about.'

'So was Kylie really in love with Zak?'

'I don't think so. I don't think she could see beyond the wedding. Zak's father insisted on paying for a grand wedding. And they were going to spend their honeymoon in the Maldives. Kylie had never been abroad before, never been on an aeroplane, never even been up to London. She couldn't talk about anything else.'

'Bit insensitive of her to talk about it to you.'

'She talked to the other girls in the office and they told me.'

'Who lives upstairs from you?' asked John, speaking for the first time.

'Marilyn Josh.'

Agatha consulted her notes. 'She works at Barrington's?'

'That's right.'

Was it Marilyn who had seen her the other night and alerted whoever it was who had tried to run her down? wondered Agatha.

'We might have a word with her afterwards,' said John. 'Is she away? She didn't answer the doorbell.'

'She sleeps late on Sunday mornings and nothing usually wakes her.'

'So,' pursued Agatha, 'what kind of girl was Kylie?'

'She was lovely to look at. I mean, you see girls like that on the telly,' said Harry, 'but you never expect to see one like that here. I couldn't believe my luck when she agreed to be my fiancée. Mind you, I was a bit worried I'd got her on the rebound.'

John and Agatha exchanged glances.

'Who was she rebounding from?' asked John.

'Mr Barrington.'

'What? The owner of Barrington's.'

'Him. Yes.'

'Wait a bit. He can't be a young man, surely, to own a firm like that.'

Harry scowled. 'He's a dirty old man, nearly fifty.'

'And not married?' asked Agatha.

'Yes, he is, but he told Kylie he would get a divorce.'

Agatha looked at Harry in amazement. 'And what did the other girls think about Kylie dating the boss?'

'They didn't know. She never told them. I knew, because I was mad about her.' He flushed an even deeper red than before. 'I used to follow her. She'd told the other girls she was taking French classes at Evesham College, so after work, she'd walk to the car park at Evesham College and he'd pick her up there.'

'And were they having an affair?'

'Kylie swore to me they'd never had an affair. He used to drive her out to restaurants in the country for dinner. He'd give her presents.'

'Like what?' asked John.

'He gave her a solid-gold necklace, that I know. She showed it to me and said she'd told her mum it was gilt.'

'So how did that end?' asked Agatha, who was rapidly revising her opinion of Kylie.

'A friend of his wife's saw them together in that Greek restaurant in Chipping Campden and told her. Turns out his wife has a lot of money and he'd never intended getting a divorce. He managed to persuade his wife that

Kylie had been thinking of leaving work and that because she was such a good worker, he had taken her out for dinner to persuade her to stay. Anyway, Kylie started going out with me. I thought all my Christmases had come. She was a beautiful girl.'

'But what was she *like*?' demanded Agatha.

'Of course, you never met her. She had a sweet face and this long blond hair and a figure like a model and . . .'

Agatha did not want to say she had once seen Kylie at the beauticians because that might give Harry a hint that she was a local. 'I'm not interested in what she looked like,' said Agatha. 'I'm interested in her character.'

Harry blinked a little, a puzzled frown between his brows. John thought that Harry had never bothered much about what Kylie was really like.

'She chattered away about the office and the girls and things like that. Girl talk, you know. She said she was ambitious. She didn't want to be stuck in Evesham for the rest of her life.'

Agatha sighed. 'But that's exactly what would have happened if she had married you. Was she a virgin?'

Harry turned red. 'That's a very personal question.'

'No harm in answering it now she's dead.'

'No, she wasn't,' he mumbled. 'She was pretty hot.'

Agatha said, 'I think we should have a word with Marilyn, seeing as how she lives above you. Do you think she'll be awake now?'

'I'll phone her.' He took a mobile phone out of his pocket and proceeded to dial. He turned a little away from them and muttered into it, but Agatha caught the gist of his remarks, which amounted to that he was with the television people and he didn't want Phyllis to know because she would muscle in on the interview.

Agatha's previous mental picture of Kylie, reinforced by the visit from her decent mother, was beginning to change. Instead of Kylie being a fresh-faced innocent, if Harry McCoy's remarks were anything to go by, Kylie had been an empty-headed little tart. Still, the girl had been murdered and no one should be allowed to get away with that.

Marilyn arrived, breathless and excited, wearing black leggings, high-heeled white sling-backed shoes, a skimpy T-shirt, and a purple fake fur jacket. Her thin shoulders were hunched and her small mouth hung perpetually open under a long nose and heavy-lidded eyes.

'Is there a hidden camera?' she asked, looking excitedly around.

'It's not *Candid Camera*,' said Agatha. 'We're just asking a few questions about the youth of Evesham in general and Kylie Stokes in particular.'

'What's your names?' asked Marilyn.

'John Armitage,' said John with a smile. 'And this is Pippa Davenport.'

He could have thought of a better name for me, thought Agatha. John took over the questioning. He started by asking her about her life. Marilyn flirted with him, giggling and punctuating her answers with hundreds of 'you knows'.

Then he said, 'Have any of you ever been in trouble over drugs?'

'Don't think so.' Marilyn looked sideways under her heavy lids at Harry. 'There's Phyllis. She's tough, you know. She could be taking something, know what I mean?'

'But no one you know has been in trouble with the police?'

Marilyn shook her head.

'How long had you all known each other?'

''Bout a year, you know. Phyllis has been with Barrington's the longest. Maybe three years. Me, a year. The others had just joined before me. New business, you know. Been building up staff ever since, you know. They was a small firm in Worcester before then, you know. Just plumbing, like. Then Mr Barrington decided to expand into bathroom fittings.'

'How old was Kylie?'

'Eighteen, same as me. She'd been working at the market with her mum when she left school at sixteen. She'd taken a computer course at the college. Said she wanted to better herself. Quite the little madam,' added Marilyn with sudden venom.

'You don't seem to have liked her,' said Agatha.

The thin shoulders under the purple jacket shrugged.

'And yet you all gave her a hen party?'

'Oh, offices, you know. You get along, have a bit of a laugh.'

'So tell me about the hen party.'

'Mr Barrington let us use the office after hours. We had drinks and a few laughs and then we dressed up Kylie in streamers and put on funny hats and walked her a bit of a way home through the town, you know. We was all a bit drunk, laughing, you know, and shouting rude remarks at the boys in the streets. Then we all split up when we got to the High Street.'

'And were there any quarrels?'

'Naw. Phyllis wasn't there.'

'Trouble maker, is she?'

'Yes, but don't you go telling her I said so. She's got a terrible temper.'

They asked her a few more questions and then parried her questions about when the programme was going to appear before taking their leave.

'There are lots of nice people in Evesham,' said Agatha as she and John walked to the car park.

'But not that lot at Barrington's,' commented John. 'Which of the girls have you still got to question separately?'

'Three of them,' groaned Agatha. 'Ann Trump, Mary Webster and Joanna Field.'

'Got their addresses?'

'Yes.'

'So let's try them.'

'You seem to be enjoying this.'

'Oh, it keeps me away from the computer and it's much more interesting than fiction.'

When they got to the car, Agatha studied her notes. 'Ann Trump lives out on the Cheltenham Road. We could try her.'

'What other stones are we going to lift up?' he asked, letting in the clutch.

'We've got to see Barrington himself.'

'Better see him at the office. Even if we find out where he lives, he won't talk easily with his wife there.'

Agatha cast a covert glance at John as he negotiated the traffic. Here she was with a very good-looking man and, instead of feeling thrilled, feeling puzzled. He was easy in her company, rather, she judged, in the way he would be relaxed with an author he met at a book convention. That was it! His behaviour towards her was like that of a business colleague. His attitude was definitely sexless. Not a frisson.

Still, Mrs Bloxby had advised her not to scare him off, to play it cool. But what did the vicar's wife know about men? thought Agatha sulkily.

They had expected to find another flat, but Ann Trump's home was a prosperous-looking villa. 'Must live with her parents,' commented John as they walked up the garden path. 'I never asked you. How are you feeling now after your fright?'

'I'm all right now. Thanks,' said Agatha. She was about to add that she felt all right during the day, but was still sleeping with the light on and waking up in a sweat at the slightest sound during the night, but he was already ringing the doorbell.

A man in golfing clothes answered the door. Agatha went into her usual television speech and desire to interview Ann Trump. He said he was Mr Trump, Ann's father, and turned away and shouted, 'Ann! That telly woman you were talking about is here!'

'I'll leave you in the lounge,' he said. 'My lady wife is out shopping and I'm off to play golf. Make yourselves comfortable.'

Agatha and John sat side by side on a green velvet-covered sofa. Looking round, Agatha decided that much of the family life must go on in the kitchen because everything in the lounge looked new and barely used. The room was cold.

A few moments after her father had left, Ann came into the room. She was fairly pretty, with a round face, wide brown eyes and dark curls.

'Like a drink?' asked Ann, going to a cocktail cabinet against the wall and opening it. The strains of 'Believe Me If All Those Endearing Young Charms' filled the room. Inside, the cabinet was lit with pink neon. Agatha noticed that the bottles were all full and glasses of different sizes neatly ranged. Obviously not a family of drinkers.

Agatha glanced at John, who shook his head. The thought flashed into her mind that if John did not drink much, there was little hope of softening him up for the kill.

'Not for us,' she said. 'Come and sit down, Ann. I decided it would be better to interview each one of you individually.'

She went on to ask Ann about her job and her hobbies and the entertainments of Evesham before getting on to the subject of Kylie's death.

'I can't think how anyone could murder her,' said Ann. 'I mean, there was nothing *to* murder.'

'What do you mean?' asked John.

'Well, she was pretty friendly towards everyone, easy to get on with.'

'Apart from Zak, did she have any boyfriends?' asked Agatha.

'She was engaged to a boy called Harry McCoy, but she dumped him for Zak.'

'Anyone else? What about any of the bosses?'

She laughed. 'Mr Barrington? No, not possible.' So Harry hadn't gossiped to the girls.

'So tell me about her engagement to Zak. Was she happy?'

Agatha looked in irritation at John, who had risen and crossed to the cocktail cabinet and was opening and shutting the lid, letting out bursts of tinkling music.

'Help yourself,' said Ann.

John regained his seat. 'I was fascinated by the mechanism.'

'You were asking about her engagement,' said Ann. 'She was ever so happy. She had a lovely diamond ring. Phyllis was mad at her, of course.' Ann blushed. 'Don't tell Phyllis I said anything. She's got a temper.'

'Yes, I gather Phyllis was dating Zak before he got engaged to Kylie.'

'Ever so cut up about it, Phyllis was,' said Ann. 'And Kylie did rather flash that ring under Phyllis's nose.'

'And yet you say there was nothing about her that would drive anyone to murder her!'

'Oh, well, girls are always quarrelling,' said Ann sententiously.

'So you don't think Phyllis could have murdered her?'

Ann giggled. 'Are you doing *Crime Watch* for the TV? Sounds like it.'

'No, no,' said Agatha quickly. 'Kylie's death intrigues me. And John Armitage here is a detective-story writer, a famous one.'

Ann surveyed John without much interest. 'Didn't think anyone read books these days, with so many channels on the telly to watch.'

'John sells millions of books,' said Agatha.

'Must be to old people,' said Ann. 'Awful lot of them around these days.'

To be on the safe side, Agatha turned her questioning back to the pleasures of the youth of Evesham and then they took their leave.

'Not much there,' said John, stifling a yawn.

He's getting bored, thought Agatha. Not surprising. Men of his age who look like him usually go after younger women. I'm getting old. Soon no one will want me.

As she got into his car, she said in a small voice, 'Maybe you've had enough.'

'Not yet. Who's left?'

'Mary Webster and Joanna Field.'

'Okay, let's get rid of one of them and have lunch.'

Agatha consulted her notes. 'Mary Webster lives in that new housing development on the Four Pools Estate. Make a left here.'

But when they got to the address Mary Webster had given them it was to find no one was at home. 'That leaves Joanna Field,' said Agatha.

Chapter Five

Joanna Field lived in a flat above a flood-damaged shop in Port Street. They rang the downstairs bell. 'I don't think they'll have any electricity yet,' said John. He tried the door. 'It's open. Let's go up.'

On the way up the stairs they could see the watermark from the flooding. John knocked at a door at the top.

It was opened by Joanna Field. So domineering had Phyllis been when Agatha had first met the girls that she had not registered then that Joanna was pretty. She had curly auburn hair and intelligent grey eyes in her smooth young face.

'Oh, it's you,' she said. 'Come in.'

'I hope we're not disturbing you,' said John. The room into which she led them was sunny and filled with a cosy clutter of books, flowers, chintz-covered furniture and the strains of Max Bruch's Violin Concerto in G Minor. Joanna switched off the music and urged them to sit down.

Agatha asked her now-usual opening questions and Joanna replied that she spent a lot of her evenings at Evesham College studying computer programming. 'I want to get on,' she said. 'My father died shortly after I was born and then my mother got ill with cancer while I was at school. I gave up a chance of getting to university to nurse her. She's dead now.'

'Sorry,' said Agatha gruffly, feeling rather shabby at involving this girl in lies about television. Determinedly she ploughed on. 'We're also interested in the death of Kylie, as you know.'

'I've been thinking about that,' said Joanna. 'I think poor Kylie was one of those people who set up their own murder.'

'How is that? I mean, what makes you say that?'

'In the old days, she would have been called a minx. She liked winding up men. She liked her bit of power and she liked money. That's the only reason she was interested in old Barrington.'

Agatha stared at her. 'You know about Barrington? I thought that was a well-kept secret. How did you find out?'

'She'd gone out to powder her nose one day and I went to her desk to look for some forms. There was a message on her computer screen. "See you tonight, lovey. Usual place. Arthur." Arthur is Mr Barrington's first name, and there's only one Arthur in the firm. After that, I noticed that he would often summon her to his office on some pretext or another and she'd come out after about half an hour with her lipstick smeared and her hair tousled.'

'You are a very observant girl,' commented John, smiling at her.

Those intelligent grey eyes turned on him. 'I'm sure I recognize you,' said Joanna. Rising, she went to the bookshelves and took out a book and looked at the photograph on the back cover. 'You're John Armitage, aren't you?'

'Yes, that's me.'

'So what's your interest in the youth of Evesham?'

To Agatha's horror, John leaned forward as Joanna sat down again and said, 'I'll tell you the truth. Agatha Raisin, here, has been employed by Kylie's mother to try to find out who killed her daughter. I am Agatha's neighbour and decided to help. Please keep this to yourself.'

'I thought there was something odd in the way you kept trying to find out about Kylie,' said Joanna. 'I tell you what. I'll ferret around and see if I can find anything for you.'

'Here's my card,' said John. 'Let me know if you hear anything.' He smiled at Joanna and she smiled back. Agatha cleared her throat with an irritated sound.

'Who do you think might have killed Kylie?' she asked. 'Zak?'

'I don't think so. I mean, Zak was besotted with her.'

Agatha's mind flashed back to the couple on

Robinson Crusoe Island. She had forgotten that Zak and Kylie had reminded her of them. But she herself had witnessed how distressed Zak was.

'What about Harry McCoy?'

'Not him either. I really don't know. Her death involved drugs. Maybe she heard something she shouldn't.'

John said, 'Well, keep your eyes and ears open. You could be of great help to us.' Again that smile.

Agatha and John rose. 'Before you leave,' said Joanna to John, 'you must sign your books.'

Agatha fidgeted impatiently while John signed four books. 'Thank you,' said Joanna and John kissed her on the cheek.

When they were both outside in the street again, Agatha muttered, 'So, Humbert Humbert, where now?'

He swung round. 'What did you say?' he demanded.

'I was wondering about lunch,' said Agatha quickly.

'We'll get a snack somewhere. What about a pub?'

'There's a quiet pub up in the High Street. The food won't be very exciting but it's never busy and we can talk there.'

Once inside The Grapes, they ordered beer and sandwiches. The sandwiches were dry and

110

curling at the edges. 'I can see why this place is quiet,' said John. 'Let's see how far we've got. Phyllis, maybe with the help of Harry McCoy, somehow lured her out of her home in her wedding gown and bumped her off. "Show us the wedding dress," that kind of thing.'

'Don't like it,' said Agatha, giving up on the sandwiches and reflecting that the ongoing battle of the middle-aged bulge was at least getting some help.

'So now we come to Barrington. He was frightened of his wife finding out. Kylie liked money, or so we gather. I wonder what this Barrington looks like. I mean, for a young girl like that to have an affair with a middle-aged man can only mean money was the attraction.'

'Exactly,' said Agatha forcefully, thinking of Joanna.

'So just suppose she was blackmailing him.'

'I wonder. I wonder if the police have looked at her bank account.'

'There's no reason for them to do so. They'd need to know about Barrington and I bet they don't.'

'We could go and see Freda Stokes,' said Agatha. 'But what reason do we give for asking to see her daughter's bank statements?'

'We could just ask to see them. She might just take it as part of the investigations. Where does she live?'

'Near Joanna. Up and round the corner by the tax office.'

'So let's go. Are you going to eat your sandwiches?'

'I can't.'

'Then let's see how we get on with Freda Stokes.'

Freda lived in a red brick terraced house. 'This is quite near where Sharon Heath lives as well,' said Agatha.

Freda Stokes answered the door. She stared at them for a minute and then smiled at Agatha. 'It is you. My! I wouldn't have thought a wig and glasses would make such a difference. Come in. I should be at work but I'm having a break.'

The small downstairs living-room into which she led them had been turned into a sort of shrine for her dead daughter. There were framed photographs of Kylie everywhere – on the table, on the walls. Kylie at school. Kylie as May Queen. Kylie as a toddler being held in the arms of a small man.

'Is that your husband?' asked Agatha, pointing to the man in the photograph.

'Yes, that's Bill. Cancer took him off when she was young.'

Agatha thought guiltily of the packet of cigarettes nestling in the depths of her handbag and once more silently vowed to give up smoking.

'Can I offer you anything? Tea?'

'Maybe in a minute,' said Agatha. 'We

wondered if we could have a look at Kylie's bank statements.'

'Why?'

'Just part of our investigations,' said John.

'And who are you?'

'Sorry,' said Agatha, and introduced John.

'I'll go and get them but I still don't see why you want them.'

As they said nothing in reply to this, Freda, after another doubtful look at them, went out. They heard her mounting the stairs.

'Nice woman,' said John. 'Do you know, for her sake, I hope there's nothing of interest in those statements.'

They waited patiently. The room grew dark, and outside, it started to rain. Rain smeared the windowpanes and a gust of wind soughed down the street outside.

At last, Freda returned with a sheaf of bank statements. Her eyes were red with fresh weeping. 'Here you are,' she said. 'I'll be back in a minute. It fair upset me going through her things.'

John separated the bank statements. 'Here. You take this lot and I'll look through these.'

They studied the statements. At first it appeared that Kylie's wage, each week, was spent soon after it had been deposited in the bank. Then John gave an exclamation and passed a statement to Agatha. 'Look at that. Fifteen thousand pounds deposited the week before her death!'

'It may not be Barrington,' said Agatha.

'Maybe it was from Zak's father to buy a trousseau or something.'

Freda came back in. 'I'll get you some tea now.'

'There's something here we should discuss first,' said Agatha. 'Fifteen thousand pounds was deposited in your daughter's account the week before her death.'

'That's not possible. Let me see it!'

Agatha held out the relevant bank statement, which Freda snatched from her.

'I don't understand,' Freda said piteously. 'She was always broke. Always asking me for money. The bank must have made a mistake.'

Agatha took a deep breath. 'I am sorry to have to tell you this, Freda, but your daughter, Kylie, was having an affair with her boss, Mr Barrington. We fear she might even have been blackmailing him.'

Freda's face was mottled with red. 'I won't listen to this filth. I'll show you. That money probably came from Terry Jensen.' She walked to the phone and dialled a number. They heard her saying hello and then asking Terry whether he had given Kylie a present of fifteen thousand pounds. The answer was obviously in the negative, for she put the phone down, shaking her head in bewilderment. Then she swung round on Agatha, her eyes glittering with rage. 'Get out of here and don't come back!'

'But, Freda –'

'Don't you Freda me. You're nothing but an

interfering old busybody. I should have listened to that Anstruther-Jones woman in your village. She stopped me after I'd called on you, saying I looked distressed and could she help. I told her why I had visited you and she said I was to be careful. That she had heard you hadn't really solved any crimes at all. It was the police that did it every time. All you ever do is just ask silly questions or dig up dirt. Well, you're not going to ruin my daughter's good name. I'm finished with you.'

Agatha backed towards the door where John was already waiting, holding it open for her. She tried to protest. 'Don't you want to know who killed your daughter?'

'OUT!' shouted Freda.

And so they left. As they walked to the car, Agatha said in a small voice. 'What now?'

'We'll see Barrington another time. Let's try Mary Webster again.'

They drove to the Four Pools Estate, off the Cheltenham Road, past Evesham College where Kylie used to meet Arthur Barrington and turned right into the housing estate opposite Safeways supermarket. 'Just there,' said Agatha, pointing to a house at the end of a row. 'Yes, that's it.'

Agatha still felt shaken after the confrontation with Freda. While she had been investigating on Freda's behalf, she had felt like a real detective. Now she felt diminished. She longed to go home and forget about the whole thing. John wasn't much company, handsome though he was. There was something almost robotic about his good looks, surely too smooth and unmarked for a man of his age. James Lacey was handsome, but in a high-nosed, rangy sort of way, and Charles was chatty. Maybe John Armitage had paid for a face-lift. As he rang the bell, she studied around his ears for any tell-tale signs until he turned and looked at her curiously with that green gaze of his that gave so little away.

The door opened. A tired, flustered woman faced them. From behind her came the wail of a baby. 'We're from television,' said Agatha. 'Is Mary Webster at home?'

The woman turned and called, 'Mary!' in a high shrill voice. Then, facing them again, she said, 'I'm ever so sorry, I can't ask you in. Mary'll need to take you somewhere.'

She stood aside as Mary appeared, pulling on a raincoat. 'Still wet, is it?' she asked.

'It's stopped now,' said John.

'Take them somewhere for a coffee,' pleaded her mother. 'Bunty needs her feed.' Another angry wail from somewhere inside the house bore out what she said.

''S awful,' grumbled Mary over her shoulder as she preceded them down the short garden path. 'Mum's too old to have more babies, but she would go and do it.'

'There's a Little Chef round the corner,' said Agatha to John. 'Let's take her there.'

Mary was a very small girl wearing very high heels. She had perky features and an upturned nose. She reminded John of illustrations of Piglet in *Winnie the Pooh*. Her eyes were small and close together and those eyes surveyed them curiously as some five minutes later they sat over cups of coffee in the Little Chef.

Feeling weary, Agatha introduced John and then asked the same questions about the amusements of the youth of Evesham before turning to Kylie's murder. 'What we really want to know at the moment,' said Agatha, 'is whether you think Kylie was taking drugs or not.'

'I know she did, just the once, like.'

'Tell us about it.'

She looked suddenly alarmed. 'This won't go out on the telly, will it? My ma would kill me.'

'No, I promise you,' said Agatha. 'Look, no tape recorder, no camera.'

'I went into the Ladies at Barrington's one day and Kylie was smoking. I said, "That cigarette smells funny." She giggled and said it was grass and would I like a puff. So we shared the joint and we was laughing all over the place. She made me promise not to tell anyone.'

'When was this?' asked John.

'Oh, would be last year.'

'Was she with Zak then?'

'No, she was engaged to Harry – Harry McCoy.'

'Did she ever tell you where she got the joint from?'

Mary shook her head. 'All I knew is that she and Harry had been clubbing in Birmingham. Probably bought some there.'

'What about heroin?' asked Agatha.

'Naw. Never a sign of the stuff. What'll I have to wear for the telly?'

'We'll be filming most of it in the disco. So whatever clothes you normally wear to that.'

'You going to give us a dress allowance?'

'I don't even get one myself.'

'I can see that,' said Mary with all the brutality of the young to the middle-aged and surveying Agatha's plain skirt, blouse and jacket. 'You should get yourself something more trendy. Make you look younger.'

'I am not in front of the cameras. I merely do the research.'

'But maybe if you did something with your appearance and got a face-lift, you could make it big-time,' went on Mary with a patronizing kindness. 'Look at Joan Collins.'

'Look at her yourself,' snarled Agatha. 'Now let's get on with this interview.'

Mary shrugged. 'You don't seem much interested in me. Only Kylie. And she's dead.'

John took over and returned to questioning Mary about her life while Agatha stifled a yawn and gazed out of the window at the passing traffic.

At last, to Agatha's relief John smiled at

Mary and said, 'That will do splendidly for the moment. Coming, Pippa?'

Agatha hurriedly remembered that was supposed to be her name. 'You'd best run me home,' Mary was saying.

They dropped her off.

'Back to the village,' said John, 'and we'll talk over what we've got. Your place or mine?'

'I thought you'd never ask,' teased Agatha flirtatiously, and then realized from his surprised look that it was a straightforward question and not an invitation to indulge in anything warmer than the murder investigation.

'Mine,' she said. 'I've got to feed the cats.'

'We'd better phone Worcester police,' said John, seated in Agatha's kitchen.

Agatha straightened up from petting her cats, and stared at him.

'Why on earth?'

'Because we've got to tell them about that bank statement.'

'I think, for the sake of Freda Stokes, we should try to protect her daughter's reputation. I mean, it may have nothing to do with Barrington.'

'Even if it has nothing to do with Barrington, it has something to do with someone. The police can ask the bank if the deposit was made by cheque and then they can find out who it was. We really can't keep this sort of information to ourselves.'

'But we've done all the work!'

'I still would feel better about it if we told the police.'

'Just one more day,' pleaded Agatha. 'We'll go and see Barrington tomorrow and then we'll go to the police.'

John frowned. 'Then we have to explain why we held on to this information.'

'We'll tell them we only just found out,' said Agatha impatiently.

'And then they'll go to Mrs Stokes for that bank statement and she'll say we knew today.'

'We'll go to Barrington first thing in the morning and then straight to the police.'

'Oh, all right. I see you've got the newspapers. Let's have a look through them and see if they've got anything.'

Agatha made coffee and they sat down opposite each other at the kitchen table and began to read. Agatha squinted down at the newsprint and then rose and took a large magnifying glass out of a kitchen drawer and returned to the table.

'You should get glasses,' said John.

'I don't need glasses,' snapped Agatha. 'The kitchen's dark.'

John shrugged and bent his head over a newspaper again.

Agatha raised the glass and looked at him through it. She found it hard to admit to herself that her sight was not nearly as good as it used to be. She noticed for the first time the lines on his forehead, down either side of his mouth and round his eyes. He looked up suddenly and she flushed guiltily and lowered the glass.

'What were you looking for?' he asked. 'Blackheads?'

'You always look so young,' said Agatha. 'Now I see you've got lines.'

'Then you do need glasses. Smoking's a sure way to ruin your eyesight and give you lots of lines around the mouth.'

Agatha's hand flew up to cover her mouth. At that moment, the sun came out and the kitchen was flooded with light. 'Nonsense,' she said, 'I can read perfectly and I haven't had a cigarette yet today.' The words were no sooner out of her mouth than she was assailed with a craving for a cigarette. 'Although I'll have one now. Any objections?'

'Go ahead. I'm not a nicotine Nazi.'

Agatha lit up a cigarette. Her head swam and it tasted dreadful, but she was addicted and so she continued to smoke until the dizziness passed.

They read steadily but there was nothing in the papers. John said he would go home and pick her up early in the morning.

Agatha opened her mouth to ask him to stay, to invite him for dinner, but remembered Mrs Bloxby's words. Maybe the vicar's wife was

121

right and she should play it cool, although what did a mere vicar's wife know about anything anyway?

Once inside his own cottage, John Armitage looked uneasily at the phone. They should have called the police. But if the police somehow got the information about the bank account today, the fact that they might have withheld information would be irrelevant.

He went out and got into his car and drove to Evesham, parked and went to a public phone-box in the High Street. He dialled the number of Worcester police. Putting on what he hoped was a Midlands accent, he said quickly, 'Check Kylie Stokes's bank account.' He quickly replaced the receiver, feeling better; feeling that he had not been quite the bad citizen Agatha Raisin wanted him to be.

On Monday morning, Agatha and John drove back to Evesham. John was silent. He felt he should tell Agatha he had tipped off the police, and yet found he could not. His ex-wife had always been marvellous at making scenes. He had a feeling that Agatha in a really nasty temper might prove to be worse than his ex.

They asked a man behind a counter who took orders and sold spare parts if they could see Mr Barrington, explaining they were from a television company. He went through to the back of the premises. It was ten minutes before he returned. 'Follow me,' he said, lifting up a flap in the counter.

They walked along a corridor until he stopped at a door, knocked and then ushered them in.

Arthur Barrington stood up behind a massive desk and held out his hand. 'I've heard you were doing research,' he said. 'It's a pleasure to meet you. Sit down.'

They sat down in two easy chairs facing the desk.

Barrington was a portly man with thinning black hair combed across his scalp in long strips. He had a fleshy, florid face and small bright eyes. The backs of his thick hands were covered in black hairs.

'What would you like to know?'

Agatha glanced at John, wanting him, for once, to take over the questioning, but John was staring straight ahead. She cleared her throat. Better cut to the chase.

'During our research,' she began, 'we became interested in the murder of Kylie Stokes. We gather she had been having an affair with you. Her bank account shows that fifteen thousand pounds was paid into her account a week before she died. Was she blackmailing you?'

Arthur Barrington got to his feet, his face red with anger. 'How dare you! Get out of here or I'll call the police.'

'Call them,' said Agatha.

He pressed a buzzer on his desk. The thick-set man they had seen at the front desk came charging through the door. 'What is it, boss?'

'Get them out of here, George. And make sure they don't come back.'

Agatha and John got up hurriedly and made for the door. They were followed down the corridor and outside by the menacing bulk of George, who then stood with his hands on his hips until they drove off.

'Where to now?' asked Agatha.

'Worcester, Agatha, and I don't care what you say; we're going to the police.'

Although Agatha had silently prayed on the road to Worcester that Detective Inspector John Brudge would not be available, her prayers were not answered, and on arrival they were taken straight to see him.

John, after explaining who he was, outlined what they had found. 'We would have come to you yesterday,' he said, 'but we thought you might be off work on Sundays.'

'I'm never off work,' said Brudge. He glared at Agatha. 'I thought I told you to keep out of this.'

'No, you didn't,' said Agatha, 'and you should be grateful to us for bringing you all this information.'

He eyed them narrowly. 'And was it one of you who phoned us anonymously yesterday evening from a public callbox in Evesham to say we ought to look at Kylie Stokes's bank account?'

'Not us,' said Agatha vehemently, and then wondered if the culprit had been John.

'You've got to stop masquerading as people from a television company or I'll need to charge you.'

'But how can we find out any more information for you if we do?' demanded Agatha.

'Look here, Mrs Raisin, we can get at the truth without your interference.'

'Oh, really? You hadn't even thought about checking her bank account.'

'Nonetheless, I can't have you duping people by pretending to be from some television company. I told you before –'

'You didn't!'

'I'm telling you now. From now on, leave things to us.'

A very chastened pair exited from police headquarters.

'You didn't tell him someone tried to kill you,' said John. 'I left it to you to tell him that.'

'I couldn't tell him,' wailed Agatha. 'That really would have been withholding information. Fortunately, you gave him the idea that we had found out everything yesterday.' She looked at him. 'Hey, was that you who gave the anonymous tip-off about Kylie's bank account?'

'Yes.'

'Well, that was a dirty trick.'

'It was on my conscience, Agatha.'

'Your conscience doesn't matter any more,' she said gloomily. 'We've been stopped in our tracks.'

'Let me think. Let's go for a drink.'

Soon, seated in a Worcester pub, they faced each other in silence. What does he think of me? wondered Agatha. Does he see me as a woman? That crack about lines round the mouth, does he find me ugly? Old? He seemed quite taken with Joanna Field. I wonder when he last had sex with anybody. I don't think I fancy him. It's just that I don't like being treated like another fellow.

'I've been thinking,' he said at last, 'that there is a way we might go on. That wig and glasses really changed your appearance. As long as you don't appear in any of the same clothes you wore when you were masquerading as Pippa, we could get away with it. Listen to this idea. The television company has dropped the idea, but I became interested in Kylie's death while helping Pippa. My next-door neighbour is a famous amateur detective. What could be more natural than us continuing the investigations?'

'Do you really think I look that different without the disguise?'

'Yes. It was a very heavy, large blond wig, and the glasses were enormous. I'm sure we could get away with it.'

'So where do we go from here? I know. I've got this friend in Mircester police, Bill Wong. I could ask him to let us know how Worcester police are getting on. He's got a friend over there.'

'That's a start. I don't think the police will get any further with Kylie's bank account. I've a feeling the money was probably paid in in cash.'

'But they'll check Barrington's bank and see if he withdrew the money.'

'True. I wish there was some way you could get to know Mrs Barrington. We can hardly go and interview her now. I wonder what her social life is like.'

'Let's go back to Evesham and look up a phone-book at the post office. We can get Barrington's home address from that.'

Arthur Barrington turned out to live in a large villa in the Greenhill area of Evesham. 'We'll park near his house,' said John, 'and watch to see if anyone who could be Mrs Barrington leaves, follow her and hope she goes somewhere to get her hair done or have a coffee or something.'

Agatha's stomach rumbled. 'Don't you ever eat?' she asked.

'I'm pretty hungry, but let's do this first.'

They parked just before Barrington's villa. It was a quiet, tree-lined street. John opened the glove compartment. 'Good, I knew I'd a bar of chocolate in here.'

'Goodie, let me have it.'

'You can have half.'

They sat eating chocolate and looking at the house.

'What do you think about?' asked Agatha.

'You mean about Barrington?'

'No, not Barrington. Things. All we ever talk about is the case.'

'What d'you want me to talk about?'

'You, for instance.'

'What else is there to know?' he demanded impatiently. 'I am divorced. I do not have any children. I write detective stories.'

'There are other things to talk about. Books. Movies.'

'Ah, books. You read *A Cruel Innocence*. You said it did not ring true. Take me through that.'

Agatha bit her lip. She did not want him to know that she had intimate knowledge of Birmingham slums.

To her relief she saw a woman driving out of the entrance to Barrington's villa.

'Look!' she cried. 'That's probably her.'

'We'll follow carefully,' he said, switching on the ignition and letting in the clutch. 'Don't want her to know she's being followed.'

'She won't know she's being followed,' Agatha pointed out. 'It's only in spy stories that they know they are being followed.'

Mrs Barrington, if it was Mrs Barrington,

drove into Evesham and parked in Merstow Green. When she emerged from her car, they saw she was slim and blond, with long tanned legs ending in trainers. She headed straight for the beauticians.

'It's the Pilates class today,' said Agatha. 'I forgot. I'll run around the corner to that cheap shop in the High Street and buy leggings and a T-shirt.'

'I'll get something as well,' said John. 'Bit of exercise would do me good.'

'I don't think there'll be room for you. But we can try.'

Ten minutes later, Rosemary welcomed them both. 'You're in luck,' she said to John. 'Two of my ladies didn't turn up. But we've done the relaxation bit.'

While they performed knee stirs, hamstring stretches and the diamond press – the last a pretty gruelling exercise – Agatha stole covert looks at Mrs Barrington. She had dyed blond hair, worn long. She was very slim and had an even tan, that faintly orange tan which comes from a bottle. Her face was only faintly lined, a long face, a Modigliani face. Her concentration was fierce. The other members of the class groaned and chatted and laughed as they performed their exercises, but her face remained throughout a mask of almost narcissistic concentration.

Hardly the sort of woman to get on chatty terms with, thought Agatha. A lot of money had gone into keeping her slim and fairly unlined. Her leotard was an expensive one.

After the class was over, John stayed behind in the exercise room while the women went into the other room to change.

'I feel better after that,' commented Agatha to Mrs Barrington. 'I don't think we've met. I'm Agatha Raisin.'

'Stephanie Barrington,' she replied with a cool look. 'Now, I must go.'

Agatha watched helplessly as Stephanie put on her coat and headed for the stairs. Agatha struggled quickly out of her leggings and T-shirt and put on her street clothes. She rushed to join John in the other room and stopped in surprise. He was chatting to Stephanie, who looked quite animated and was saying, 'But I've read all your books.'

Over her shoulder – her slim back was to Agatha – John gave Agatha a dismissive roll of the eyeballs.

She went reluctantly downstairs. Now what was she supposed to do? She couldn't sit in the car. John had the keys.

She stood behind the shelter of the car and finally saw them emerge. They stood talking for a while on the pavement and then, to her relief, John headed towards the car park.

'So how did you get on?' demanded Agatha impatiently.

'I'm giving her dinner tonight,' he said triumphantly.

'Where?'

'My place.'

'Can I come?'

'Bad idea. She wants to talk to me about writing a book. She won't talk freely with you around.'

'When her husband knows who it is she's meeting, he'll put a stop to it. He'll remember you from this morning.'

'He won't know. She said he sneers at everything she does, so she's not going to tell him.'

'Fancy you, does she?'

'Oh, yes.'

'Wouldn't fancy her a bit, if I were a man,' said Agatha as they drove off. 'Looks a cold fish.'

He grinned. 'I am sure she has hidden passions.'

That evening, Agatha fretted alone. She did not have a crush on John, and yet she resented his interest in other women like Joanna Field and now Stephanie Barrington. Of course, it had all to do with the case. She decided to visit Mrs Bloxby.

Mrs Bloxby listened carefully to Agatha's adventures and then said, 'You are very, very lucky the police did not book you for impersonating a television researcher.'

'They've got enough to do. I found things out for them they wouldn't have known otherwise and I wasn't conning anyone out of money.'

'So he's with this Stephanie Barrington at the moment?'

'Yes.' Agatha looked sour. 'Okay, he's a handsome man. I haven't made a pass at him once. But it is galling that he doesn't seem to see me as a woman.'

'Come, now. You surely don't want another involvement after all you've been through.'

'It makes me feel ugly and unwanted,' said Agatha in a small voice.

'Agatha, you are not a teenager any more. You are a mature woman. You should be able to think well of your appearance without needing some man to make you feel good.'

'I know, I know, but that's the way it is.'

'It looks very much as if this Mr Barrington might be the murderer.'

'I suppose. I'm losing interest. Thanks for listening. I may as well have an early night.'

'Wait a minute. I've got something for you.'

Mrs Bloxby walked off into the kitchen and came back carrying a casserole. 'Here you are, some of my lamb casserole with dumplings. I don't think you're eating properly.'

'Thanks,' said Agatha. 'I haven't been eating much at all.'

She carried the casserole back to her cottage, noticing as she walked along Lilac Lane that

Stephanie's car was not parked outside John's cottage.

Agatha put the casserole down on the kitchen table. She phoned him.

'Oh, Agatha,' he said. 'I did try to call you. She just didn't show up.'

'Mrs Bloxby's given me a lamb casserole and there seems loads there, enough for two. Want some?'

'That's kind of you, but I've already eaten, and I should really get started on a new book. See you around. Bye.'

Agatha slowly replaced the receiver. So that was that. She heated the casserole, helped herself to a plate of it, and filled two small dishes for her cats.

The doorbell rang. Agatha leaped to her feet. John!

But when she opened the door, Mrs Anstruther-Jones was standing there. 'What is it?' demanded Agatha rudely.

'May I come in? I want to ask you a favour.'

'All right.'

Agatha turned and walked indoors and Mrs Anstruther-Jones followed her. 'So what is it?' asked Agatha again.

'It's the oddest thing. I knew this chap when I was very young. Tom Clarence. He's phoned up and wants me to meet him in Evesham for a late drink.' She giggled. 'I used to be awfully keen on him. He's married. I'm meeting him at the Evesham Hotel.'

'So what's it got to do with me?'

'Well, him being married and all. I don't want to be recognized.'

'So?'

'I wondered if I could borrow that blond wig of yours and the glasses. Sort of a disguise.'

'Sure,' said Agatha, suddenly weary. 'I won't be needing either. I'll get them for you.'

She went up to her bedroom. What a life, she thought, as she picked up the wig and glasses. Even an old trout like Anstruther-Jones has a date.

She went downstairs and shoved them at her. 'Have fun.'

'You won't tell anyone?'

'No.'

Mrs Anstruther-Jones giggled again. 'You must be so used to these sorts of liaisons,' she said, and before Agatha could think of a reply, she headed out of the cottage.

Agatha slammed the door after her.

She did not know that she would never see Mrs Anstruther-Jones again.

Chapter Six

Agatha awoke next morning to a sunny day and restored spirits. She would forget about the case and phone Roy in London and see if there was any freelance work on offer to keep her busy. She looked out of her kitchen window. The garden seemed to be one green mass of weeds. Normally, she would have asked Joe Blythe, a village local who charged high rates for painfully slow work, but the realization – if Roy had nothing for her – that she was facing a prospect of inactivity, spurred her to find a hoe, put on gardening gloves and get down to the task of doing the weeding herself.

Her cats curled around her legs in the warm sunlight in a rare show of affection. Perhaps if I turned into a real village woman, pottering around the house and garden all day, my cats would appreciate it, thought Agatha. She should never have become involved in trying to solve Kylie's murder. Somehow, John's very lack of response to her as a woman had undermined her confidence and she felt that when it came to detective work she was nothing more than a bumbling amateur. She was just working the tough roots of a dandelion out of the soil when she heard her doorbell ring.

Agatha sat back on her heels, debating whether to answer it. In the days of James Lacey, she would have run to the door, her heart bursting with hope. But even the thought that it might be John did not move her. The bell went again, and faintly she heard a voice shouting, 'Police!'

Now what? Agatha got to her feet and made her way quickly through the house. She opened the door just as the bell shrilled again. Detective Inspector Brudge stood there, flanked by a policewoman and a plain-clothes officer.

Agatha led them into the living-room. 'Where were you last night?' demanded Brudge.

'Why?'

'Just answer the question.'

'I've often seen this on television and I didn't believe it happened in real life,' said Agatha. 'No, I won't just answer the question until you tell me what this is about.'

They locked eyes for a long moment, then he shrugged. 'Mrs Anstruther-Jones was found dead in the early hours of this morning.'

The wig, the glasses, thought Agatha desperately. Did someone mistake her for me?

'How was she killed?'

'Hit and run.'

'Where?'

'On Waterside. May we have your movements for last night?'

'I came back here late afternoon,' said Agatha. 'I went to visit Mrs Bloxby, the vicar's wife.'

'At what time?'

'Oh, around seven o'clock. I'm not sure. We talked for a bit. Then I came back here.' Agatha steeled herself. 'Mrs Anstruther-Jones called on me.'

'Time?'

'Again I'm not sure. Ten, maybe.'

'And what did she want?'

'She was meeting an old flame. She wanted to borrow my blond wig and glasses. She said he was married and she was meeting him for a late drink at the Evesham Hotel and didn't want to be recognized. I gave them to her.'

'So what was she doing walking along Waterside? Why not park at the Evesham Hotel?'

'I would guess,' said Agatha, 'that she was enjoying the secrecy of meeting a married man for a drink. She giggled a lot. I think she probably parked on Waterside so that she could walk up to the hotel.'

There was a silence. Then Agatha asked, 'How do you know it was a hit and run? And if it took place on Waterside, why was the body not found until the early hours of the morning?'

'She had been thrown clear over some bushes. You must see the obvious, Mrs Raisin.

In the dark and with the wig and glasses, someone obviously mistook her for you. Have you told me everything you know about the Kylie Stokes case?'

'Yes,' said Agatha. She could not tell him now, at this late date, about the attempt on her life.

'We'd better take time and go over everything – and I mean, everything – you know again. Someone obviously thinks you do know something that might incriminate him.'

So Agatha talked and talked. The policewoman took notes in rapid shorthand. The cats, sensing Agatha's distress, coiled around her ankles.

And then a policeman appeared in the room, escorting John Armitage. Oh, God, thought Agatha. I must do something. He might tell them that I was nearly the victim of a hit and run.

'Sit down, Mr Armitage,' said Brudge. John sat down next to Agatha on the sofa.

He outlined what had happened to Mrs Anstruther-Jones. John gave an exclamation and turned to Agatha. 'Why, that's what . . .'

Agatha threw herself into his arms and kissed him on the mouth. 'Don't tell them,' she mumbled against his lips, and then drew away, saying, 'Oh, darling. I am so frightened. I lent her my wig and glasses and somebody obviously thought it was me.'

John looked at Agatha impassively and then

turned to Brudge. 'I suppose you want to know where I was last night?'

'More than that. I want to know everything you have found out. You have been investigating a murder with Mrs Raisin here. Somebody obviously finds her a threat. Let's go over again what you've got.'

While John talked, Agatha nervously fingered her lips. She found that one sturdy hair was growing just above her upper lip and blushed red with mortification. Had he felt it? Should she excuse herself and run up to the bathroom and yank it out? But if she left the room, and without her controlling presence, John might let slip about the attempt on her life.

Such was her worry about that hair that she could hardly feel all the fear she should have been feeling about what had been another attempt on her life.

Brudge turned back to her. 'Did Mrs Anstruther-Jones tell you who she was meeting?'

'Tom someone,' said Agatha, 'I know – Tom Clarence.'

Brudge said to his detective, 'Get on to that right away. He might still be there. Now, Mrs Raisin, I have warned you before and I am warning you again – no more amateur investigation. If it weren't for you, that woman would still be alive. If you plan to leave the area, you must let us know where you are going. The same goes for you, Mr Armitage. You will now accompany us to headquarters, where you will both make formal statements.'

'I'll just go to the bathroom first,' said Agatha. She fled up the stairs and into the bathroom, found a pair of tweezers and yanked the offending hair out. Damn middle age and all its indignities.

John and Agatha had followed the police cars to Worcester. After they had given their statements and were making their way back to Carsely, John said stiffly, 'I'll drop you off and then I really ought to get down to some work.'

'I wasn't making a pass at you,' said Agatha, studying his stern profile. 'I was trying to shut you up from saying anything about the attempt on my life.'

'I gathered that. Nonetheless, I do have to work and we have been told not to interfere any more. That poor woman. What a mess!'

Agatha realized that the only connection she had with John was Kylie's murder. Now he would no longer have time for her.

It must have been that hair, she thought. He must have felt it and got a disgust of me. The world is full of young, pretty, smooth-skinned women; why should he even look at me?

She gave a strangled sob.

'There, now,' said John. 'Don't cry. I know you must be feeling dreadfully guilty about poor Mrs Anstruther-Jones's death. But you lent her the disguise in good faith.'

And Agatha now did feel guilty about the fact that she was sobbing over middle-aged vanity and not Mrs Anstruther-Jones's death.

She blew her nose defiantly and then said, 'I wonder how the police got on with Barrington.'

'We may never know now,' said John, underlining the fact that as far as he was concerned, the case was closed.

Later that day Agatha decided to go and see Mrs Bloxby. The vicar's wife greeted her, exclaiming, 'I heard it on the news. Poor Mrs Anstruther-Jones.'

'It's worse than you know,' said Agatha, following her in. She told her about the wig and glasses.

'If she hadn't been so very silly, it wouldn't have happened,' said Mrs Bloxby. 'Have you eaten?'

'Not yet.'

'It's a lovely day. Go into the garden and have a cigarette and I'll bring you something.'

Agatha went out to a table in the garden and sat on a rustic seat under the shade of a magnificent wisteria which hung down over a pergola. Mrs Bloxby had a magic touch with flowers and the garden was a riot of daffodils, tulips, impatiens and a late-flowering cherry tree whose blossoms were rising and drifting on the lightest of breezes.

The garden bordered the churchyard where ancient stones leaned this way and that among the tussocky grass.

Mrs Bloxby emerged bearing a tray with a glass of chilled wine and a plate of ham salad, saying, 'There you are. You'll feel better when you've had something.'

As Agatha ate, Mrs Bloxby said, 'Yes, she didn't have to wear the wig and glasses. You say she was going to meet an old school friend? So why the secrecy? She envied you, you know. I think she wanted to be like you.'

'That makes me feel worse,' groaned Agatha. 'Now the police have told me very firmly to back off and John doesn't want to have anything to do with me and I think it's because I kissed him.'

'Oh, Mrs Raisin!'

'No, it's not what you think. I was trying to warn him not to tell the police something. But you see, I'd got this hair growing above my upper lip and maybe he felt it against his skin and got disgusted.'

The vicar's wife emitted an odd sound. Agatha glared at her. Were Mrs Bloxby not such a lady, Agatha could have sworn she actually sniggered.

'Mrs Raisin, here is a man who has just learned that a woman who used to visit him as much as she could has been brutally killed.

Then you kiss him. I really don't think he would have noticed if you'd had a full beard.'

'May I stay here for a bit?' asked Agatha. 'I don't feel like going back to my place. I let the cats out into the garden before I went to Worcester and they've been fed.'

'Stay as long as you like,' said Mrs Bloxby, and then started guiltily as she heard her husband arriving home.

She rose hurriedly to her feet. 'Back in a minute.'

Agatha heard the murmur of voices. Then she heard the vicar exclaim, 'That wretched woman is nothing but trouble.'

Mrs Bloxby returned to the garden just as Agatha heard the vicar's study door slam.

'On second thoughts, I'd better be going.'

'Oh, do stay.'

'No, I planned to phone Roy Silver and see if there was any freelance work going. I never got round to it. I'll go home and do it now. Keep myself occupied.'

A sad Agatha walked along to her cottage. Nobody liked her and nobody wanted her.

She was just turning into Lilac Lane when she saw Joanna Field going into John's cottage.

She hesitated. Should she join them? What had Joanna found out?

Probably nothing, she thought sourly. Just finding some excuse to call on him.

Agatha decided to check her face for any other hairs and then put on a face-pack. The green goo was just beginning to harden when the doorbell rang.

She splashed water on her face and scrubbed it with a clean towel, and then ran downstairs.

Agatha opened the door to find John and Joanna there. 'Why aren't you at work?' she asked Joanna.

'We were all sent home early.'

'Joanna has some interesting news.' John smiled. 'You've got little patches of some green stuff on your face.'

'Go into the kitchen,' said Agatha. 'Back in a minute.'

She rushed upstairs again and this time looked in her magnifying mirror. Sure enough, there were little bits of green stuck to various parts of her face.

I need glasses, came the thought, but she quickly dismissed it. She washed and creamed her face and washed it again. Carefully she applied make-up before going back down to join them.

Joanna was wearing figure-hugging trousers in a biscuit colour and she had a crisp white blouse tied at her slim waist. John was wearing a blue shirt and blue cords in a soft material. Despite the difference in their ages, they looked to Agatha's jaundiced eyes very much a couple.

'Coffee?' she asked.

'Wait till you hear Joanna's news first,' said John.

Agatha joined them at the kitchen table and smiled at Joanna. I will not be jealous, she told herself firmly.

'It's like this,' said Joanna. 'Barrington was taken away on Sunday evening by the police.'

'How do you know this?'

'Wait. We didn't know about it until yesterday, when Mrs Barrington burst into our room at the office. She was raging. She said, "Have any other of you sluts been having an affair with my husband and trying to blackmail him?" Then she began to cry and it all came out. The police had taken him away for questioning. He'd spun her some story that they wanted to know more about Kylie's friends. Then this morning they were back again and took him away again and this time she learned about Kylie blackmailing her husband. Well, we gave her tea and soothed her down. Phyllis added fuel to the fire by saying that she knew something had been going on when she didn't know a thing. Mrs Barrington ended up saying she'd had enough of him and would divorce him.'

'Did she think he might have killed her?'

'That's just it,' said Joanna, her eyes glowing. 'She said he could be very violent and she's sure he did it and she's going to tell the police that!'

'There's only one problem with that,' said Agatha. 'Why kill Kylie and in such an elaborate way *after* he had paid out the money?'

'Perhaps,' said John, 'because she'd asked for even more.'

'And what about Mrs Anstruther-Jones?'

'I think our murderer happened to be driving along and just saw her, the way he saw you. He recognized the fair hair and glasses and gunned the engine.'

'What do you mean, "the way he saw you"?' asked Joanna.

Agatha shot John a repressive look and said quickly, 'Just what he said. He means the murderer thought Mrs Anstruther-Jones was me.'

'How exciting!'

How exciting to be young and not have anyone out to kill you, thought Agatha. Then she had an awful idea. 'What if the police release the fact that the killer thought she was me? What if they bring out all that stuff about me masquerading as representing a television company? Then everyone will know my true identity and whoever it is could come here looking for me.'

'I don't think they'll do that,' said John slowly. 'Brudge won't want to let his superiors know that he didn't do much to stop you investigating. No, I don't think they'll do that.'

They discussed the case this way and that without getting any further. Then Joanna said, 'I'd best go home now. I'm a bit hungry and haven't had anything to eat yet.'

'I'll take you for something,' said John.

'Would you?' Joanna beamed. 'That's very kind.'

Surely, thought Agatha, they are not going to leave me. Surely they are not going to just go off together without including me in the invitation.

But John said, 'See you later.' They walked out. That was that.

Agatha began to feel very angry indeed. They both knew that a woman had been killed because she had been mistaken for her. It was *her* case, too, dammit.

She would phone Roy, see if there was any work, and leave for London. She looked down at the kitchen floor to find her two cats staring up at her. She felt a pang. It would mean leaving them, the only friends she had got.

She heard the doorbell ring. Ah, come to their senses, had they?

But it was Bill Wong.

'What's all this I've been hearing?' he demanded. 'My friend at Worcester police tells me that the woman who was killed last night was wearing your wig and glasses.'

'Want to go out for dinner and I'll tell you about it?'

'All right. I've a free evening.'

'We'll go to the Marsh Goose and I'll sit down and tell you everything.'

When they were seated at a table by the window in the Marsh Goose in Moreton-in-Marsh, Agatha saw John and Joan at another table across the room. They waved to her. She ignored them. 'Let's order first,' said Agatha, 'then I'll begin at the beginning and go on to the end. Damn, I feel like getting drunk tonight, but I've got to drive you back after dinner and then you've got to drive to Cirencester.'

'Them's the laws.' Bill's almond eyes crinkled with amusement in his smooth young face. The next time I get interested in some man, thought Agatha, I'll make sure he is more wrinkled than I am.

They ordered their food and then Agatha began to tell him everything that she knew and everything that had happened – with one exception. She did not tell him about the attempt on her life. He listened carefully. Then he said, 'Barrington's got a cast-iron alibi. After he was released by the police the first time he was taken in, he phoned his wife and said he was dashing off to Birmingham to see a client. He did dash off to Birmingham, but to a hotel, where he spent the night with a Miss Betty Dicks.'

'Who's she?'

'Some Birmingham secretary who he has been seducing with promises that he's ready to leave his wife any day now. He left Birmingham early in the morning to get to his work in Evesham but he went home first, where he found the police waiting for him. So he could not have killed Mrs Anstruther-Jones.'

'But he could have killed Kylie.'

'Doubtful. Whoever killed Kylie is now scared enough to want you out of the way. Have they offered you police protection?'

Agatha shook her head. 'I think they're so mad at me for interfering in police business that they don't care if someone does bump me off.'

'Either that or they're convinced that whoever killed Mrs Anstruther-Jones still thinks you are researching for television. If they, or he, or she, or whoever knew your real identity, they would have made an attempt on your life in Carsely. No, our murderer saw what he thought was you, walking along Waterside.'

'Cars!' said Agatha. 'Do any of those girls have a car?'

'Phyllis has an old Volkswagen, Ann Trump a Ford Metro, and Marilyn Josh uses Harry McCoy's old Rover. Zak and his father both have cars. You said you upset Mrs Stokes. She drives a station wagon. They're all being checked out. The police will be appealing for witnesses on television tonight. You know what ties Kylie's death and Mrs Anstruther-Jones's death together?'

'No, what?'

'Panic. There's panic in both cases. Take the case of Kylie. She's injected with an overdose of heroin. The body's dumped in some sort of freezer. It could have stayed there for weeks, months – years, even. But no, whoever did it panicked, took the body out and threw it in the river. And someone saw what they thought was you and without worrying about possible witnesses, they stamp their foot down on the accelerator.'

Agatha looked at him thoughtfully. She longed to tell him of the attempt on her life.

'What?' said Bill, looking at her quizzically. 'You haven't told me all. You're holding back something.'

'If I tell you, you'll tell the police.'

'That bad?'

'Yes, that bad.'

He looked around the restaurant. The tables were spaced well apart.

'I think you'd better tell me. Okay, I won't tell the police. Something's happened, and knowing you, it's something dangerous.'

'It's like this. I went to try to see Harry McCoy. He wasn't at home. I turned to walk back to Merstow Green car park, along Horres Street. The street was deserted. I heard the sound of a car and I don't know why I knew it was coming for me, but I threw myself over a garden hedge just as it roared past.'

'Agatha, why didn't you tell the police?'

'Because I was in my disguise of television researcher and I thought they'd make a fuss and stop me investigating. It seems silly now, but I've left it too long.' She looked up impatiently. John and Joanna were standing next to their table, smiling down at her.

'We wondered if you would like to join us in the lounge for coffee?' said John.

Agatha gave them both a basilisk look. 'No, go away.'

'That was very rude of you, Agatha,' said Bill severely.

'That was my neighbour, John Armitage, and one of the girls from Barrington's, Joanna Field.'

'So what gives? I thought you and this John were investigating together.'

'Joanna and John came round. Joanna was full of the news that Mrs Barrington had turned up and made a scene in the office, I told you that. But then she said she was hungry, John invites her out for dinner, and they both swan off without even offering to take me along.'

'Maybe he thought she would talk more freely without you around. Anyway, this attempt on your life. I think the murder of Mrs Anstruther-Jones was chance. She just happened to have been spotted. But I can't think that the attempt on Horres Street was chance. Cars don't normally drive through it going anywhere at night, but they do drive along Waterside. Are you sure there was no one at home? You say that Marilyn Josh lives there in the upstairs flat and that Phyllis is having an affair with Harry McCoy. One of them could have been at home, looked out of the window and seen you, and phoned someone. Or there's a lane at the back of Horres Street. One of them could have nipped out the back way, run round, got into a car and headed for you. That's what's so baffling. I keep getting a feeling of panic combined with amateurism. I could swear that whoever's doing this hasn't got a record, has never killed before.'

They discussed everything over and over again without coming to any firm idea of who might have done it.

When they had finished their meal and were driving back, Bill said, 'I can tell you're not in love with this John Armitage.'

'No, I'm not.'

'Well, there's no use flying off the handle with someone who isn't a boyfriend, is there? Yes, they should have invited you, but I'll bet John thought he might have been able to get more out of her without you. I told you that already. You've been involved with men since I've known you who've treated you badly, so you automatically think any man is rejecting you. Forget it, Agatha. It's bad policy to quarrel with neighbours anyway.'

'I'll think about it,' said Agatha sulkily. 'Want to come in for more coffee?'

'No, I'd best be getting back. Mother sits up until I get home.'

Agatha, not for the first time, wanted to point out to him that his mother was a possessive bag who drove off all his young girlfriends, but she knew Bill would be deeply hurt. He adored his parents.

She said goodnight to him and waved him goodbye and went indoors. A few minutes later, there was a ring at the door. She looked through the spyhole. John Armitage.

Let him rot, thought Agatha mulishly.

Chapter Seven

Agatha awoke next morning to find a letter pushed through her door. She opened it while Boswell dug his claws into the hem of her housecoat and tugged hard. She carried it into the kitchen, dragging the cat along with her.

Agatha sat down and, after dislodging Boswell's claws from her housecoat, she opened the envelope, noticing as she did so that it was unstamped.

'Dear Agatha,' she read, 'I am so sorry about last night. I could see that you were angry because I had not included you in the invitation to dinner. I thought that perhaps Joanna would tell me some more details if we were on our own. As it turned out, she had nothing new to add. Yours, John.'

Agatha felt she had been churlish. It might be an idea to phone Roy Silver first and ask about work. But she would not rush next door immediately. She would take her time and read the morning papers.

In a copy of the morning *Bugle*, she found an

article by a celebrity who had given up smoking through hypnosis. 'It worked,' Agatha read. 'The first thing I noticed was that I had more energy. Then friends started commenting on the clearness of my skin. I'm so glad I quit. My looks are important to me. You can always tell a middle-aged woman who smokes. They've got these nasty wrinkles on their upper lips. I didn't want to end up like that.'

Agatha's hand strayed nervously to her upper lip. She remembered she had the phone number of a hypnotist in Gloucester. She had always been meaning to go, but had kept putting it off. She phoned the hypnotist, who said he could see her if she could be at his consulting rooms in an hour and a half's time, as he had just received a cancellation. Agatha agreed to be there and then rushed to get ready. The day was dry but misty. Agatha drove steadily through a grey world. Water dripped from the trees beside the road.

She managed to find a parking place near the hypnotist's consulting rooms. She was five minutes early, so she celebrated with what she swore would be her last cigarette.

Half an hour later, it was all over. He had told her that from now on every cigarette she smoked would taste terrible, like burning rubber.

With a feeling of having actually done something for her health and well-being, she drove back home.

As she parked outside her cottage, she saw a familiar figure standing on her doorstep. Freda Stokes. What now? thought Agatha as she got out of the car. Another row? She pinned a smile of welcome on her face.

Freda greeted her with a cry of 'Oh, Agatha. I'm so sorry.'

'Come inside,' said Agatha, opening the door. 'Come through to the kitchen. Sit down. I'll make some coffee.'

Agatha plugged in the percolator and sat down at the kitchen table opposite Freda.

'I didn't want to believe what you told me. I *couldn't* believe what you told me,' said Freda. 'The police called on me. Mr Barrington has admitted paying Kylie – my Kylie! – to keep her quiet. I'm beginning to wonder if I knew my daughter at all. She was always like a child to me. Innocent. "I'm not like those other girls, Mum," she'd say. "I don't sleep around. I'm saving myself for my wedding day."'

'Did she need a lot of money?' asked Agatha, wondering if Kylie had indeed had a drug habit.

'She was always asking me for money. It was a bit hard for me, for I don't make that much. But she was my only child. I couldn't refuse her. Now I remember things about her, like she would wear clothes for a few months and then take them back to the shop and try to get her money back. She had this raincoat, oh, for about eight months, and she took it back to the shop and tried to say she had just bought it. But they wouldn't take it back. So she asked me to take it to the dry-cleaners. I did that and gave her the coat. She took it into her bedroom and then she came out with it and it was covered in grease spots. She said the cleaners had ruined it and I had to take it to them and demand the price of the coat. They paid up in the end but they accused me of having put the grease stains on myself. They said there was no way it could have happened otherwise.' Freda looked tearfully at Agatha. 'Do you think Kylie was *greedy*?'

'Perhaps,' said Agatha cautiously.

'And then there were times when there was money missing from my purse. I had a young girl working at the stall with me during the school holidays. I thought it must be her and fired her. Now I think it might have been Kylie. Where did I go wrong?'

By pretending nothing was happening, thought Agatha.

Aloud she said, 'I have to ask you this. Do you think she'd been taking drugs?'

'No! But then, I didn't know about the blackmail or anything,' wailed Freda. 'Maybe she took that overdose herself and the people that gave her the stuff panicked.'

'That's possible except for the fact that she was wearing that wedding dress and slipped out late at night. Someone asked her to let them see it.'

Agatha stood up and poured two mugs of coffee and put one, along with milk and sugar, in front of Freda. 'Was she very proud of the wedding dress?'

'No, that's the thing. It was my sister, Josie's, girl's gown. Josie's daughter, Iris, had only worn it once and it cost Josie a mint. Lovely gown, it was. Kylie said she wanted a new one, but I dug my heels in on that. What's the point, I said to her, of paying out all that money on a gown you'll only be wearing once? And then Iris and Kylie were the same size.'

Agatha's interest quickened. 'If she was worried about it, she might have said to someone that she didn't want to wear it and they said, "Well, bring it round and let me have a look." That suggests another woman. When she got home, did she make a phone call or have any phone calls?'

'She went straight to her room and then I heard her playing a CD. She had a mobile phone. But the police took that away and checked all phone calls to and from the house. She didn't make a phone call that evening.'

'Does this mean you want me to go on investigating?' asked Agatha.

'Yes, please. I feel I know the worst about my daughter now and nothing else can shock me.'

'Did she keep a diary?'

'No. I bought her one once, but she never bothered to write anything in it.'

'Letters from anyone?'

'None of those. Young people seem to use the phone these days.'

'I'll keep in touch with you,' said Agatha. 'I'll do my best, but the police have warned me off.'

After Freda had left, Agatha phoned John Armitage. 'You'd better drop round,' she said. 'There's been a new development.'

When John arrived, Agatha told him about the visit from Freda and what she had said.

'We need to find out more about that hen party,' said John. 'We need to find out if one of them volunteered to look at the dress, and there's another thing.'

'What?'

'No phone calls. But what about e-mails? Someone could have sent her an e-mail to her address at the firm. Joanna could check that for us.'

'Oh, her,' said Agatha.

'Yes, her. She's bright and she's clever and she knows your real identity, which the other girls don't. I don't chase young girls, Agatha.'

'I'm not interested if you do,' said Agatha crossly. She automatically lit up a cigarette and then scowled in distaste and stubbed it out.

'What's up?'

'I went to a hypnotist,' said Agatha. 'He said every cigarette I would now smoke would taste like burning rubber and he was right.'

John burst out laughing. 'There's one thing about you, Agatha – no one could ever call you boring.'

'That's me. A laugh a minute,' said Agatha gloomily.

'And I'll take you for lunch to make up for last night.'

Agatha brightened. 'I'll go and change while you phone Joanna.'

She went upstairs and changed into a trouser suit and a tailored blouse, noticing with delight that the trouser waistline was quite loose. She carefully made up her face and sprayed herself liberally with Champagne perfume before going downstairs to join him.

'Joanna said she would check Kylie's machine after all the others have gone for the night. If we wait round the corner in the Little Chef, she'll join us there about seven o'clock this evening.'

'Aren't you coming, Joanna?' demanded Marilyn Josh as the other girls put on their coats.

'I've just got a couple of bills to send out,' said Joanna. 'I'd better get them done now.'

'Please yourself,' said Phyllis nastily. 'But it's no use sucking up to the boss. He's not in.'

Joanna shrugged and pretended to concentrate on her computer. It was, she thought uneasily, as if the others suspected she was up to something. They seemed to take a long time to leave. She stayed at her desk until she heard them all disappear at last into the night. Then, just as she was about to rise from her desk, Sharon Heath came back in. 'Still here?' she said. 'Won't be a mo. I left something in me desk.'

Joanna typed steadily, glad she had taken the precaution of leaving her computer switched on. She heard Sharon behind her, opening and shutting drawers and muttering, 'Now, where did I put that dratted thing?' Then a grunt of satisfaction. 'See ya,' said Sharon. The office door banged shut and Joanna could hear her high heels clacking off down the corridor.

She had a sudden impulse to shut down her computer and leave. The silence of the office seemed threatening. But if she found something, John would be pleased with her. He *was* very attractive. She wondered if there was anything going on between him and that Raisin woman. No. Definitely not. No vibes there. She had enjoyed her dinner with him. Older men were so much more attractive. She cocked her head to one side and listened. She rose again. She heard footsteps in the corridor and sat down again hurriedly. The door opened. George, who manned the front desk, put his head round the door. 'I want to lock up. How long you going to be?'

'Give me five minutes,' said Joanna.

'Right. Give me a shout on your way out.'

She waited again until all was silent. Get on with it, she told herself.

Joanna took a deep breath and crossed the office floor to Kylie's desk. She switched on the computer.

The screen lit up, bright blue. 'Hurry up and warm up,' urged Joanna. She got into the e-mail and began to read. 'Ah, now we have it,' she said.

The blow that struck her on the back of the head was vicious and sudden. She slumped forward on the keyboard.

Agatha and John fidgeted restlessly in the Little Chef. 'It's now seven-thirty,' said John. 'She's had plenty of time. I hope nothing's gone wrong.'

'I'll wait here,' said Agatha. 'Why don't you drive along past Barrington's and see if there's still a light on in the office.'

John left and Agatha waited anxiously. What if John decided to take Joanna off on his own again with the excuse that he'd get more out of her that way? I should have given him my mobile phone number, she thought.

She waited ten minutes and then sighed with relief as she saw John's car turning into the car park once more.

He sat down and leaned forward and said urgently, 'There was an ambulance. She was being carried out.'

'Dead? Oh, God, not dead.'

'No, there was breathing apparatus over her face. The police were there and that George fellow was talking to them. They didn't see me. What with the ambulance and the police cars, a crowd had already gathered. I stood at the back.'

'We'll need to find out which hospital they've taken her to.'

'Where would that be? Here in Evesham? Worcester? Redditch? Have you got your phone?'

'In my bag.' Agatha opened her handbag, took out her mobile phone and handed it to him.

She fretted and fidgeted as he made several phone calls.

'It's early yet,' she finally interrupted him. 'She may not have arrived at whatever hospital they've taken her to. Let's go home and then try again.'

John tried again from Agatha's cottage. At last he found out that Joanna had been taken to the Alexandra Hospital in Redditch. Agatha was all for rushing there, but John said, 'We should wait until the morning.'

'Did they say what was up with her?'

'No, just that she had been admitted.'

Agatha gave a click of annoyance and took the phone from him. She dialled the Alexandra

Hospital, introduced herself as Joanna's aunt and asked to be put through to the sister in charge of the ward where Joanna was.

She asked several sharp questions and then put the phone down. 'She's got a bad concussion and is not allowed visitors until further notice. Now what do we do?'

'There's nothing we can do. In fact I think we've done enough. We should never have involved that poor girl.'

'And I can't question the other girls now that I've given up my disguise. You'll need to do that.'

'Agatha, one woman is dead and another concussed. All we seem to do is put innocent people in peril.'

'But will the police guess about checking Kylie's e-mail?'

'We can hardly phone them up now. They told us to stay out of it.'

'And I can't phone Bill Wong, you know, my detective friend. He would be very angry with us. I know, Freda Stokes. I told you we had been forgiven. She could suggest it to the police.'

Agatha went through to the living room to phone. John sat in the kitchen and waited. Books were easier. You didn't have a conscience about people who got hurt or killed in books.

He waited uneasily until Agatha came back. 'Fine, I told her. She said she'd wait until it was on the news and phone them then. It all looks bad for Barrington. I wonder if that alibi of his is foolproof.'

'He could have killed Kylie, but why would he sneak out of a Birmingham hotel and go cruising the streets of Evesham in the hope of running you over?'

'True,' said Agatha moodily. 'It all comes back to those girls. They must have known she was staying on in the office. One of them could have been suspicious, crept back, and hit her.'

'Oh, Lord. I just remembered, Agatha, there are security cameras at the entrance to Barrington's. Not only will the police be able to check who came and who went but they will also have a clear picture of the crowd watching the ambulance. They might have a good shot of my face and come demanding to know why I was there.'

'You just stick to your guns and say that you were driving past to meet me at the Little Chef when you saw the crowd, the police cars and the ambulance and stopped and got out to have a look.'

'I hate this lying. Did you never think of joining the police force and being legit?'

'I'm too old.'

'So what now? I think we should just get on with our lives and leave the mess to the police.'

'I suppose so. I feel like phoning up my friend, Roy Silver, and seeing if there's any work for me.'

'Like what?'

'Like in public relations. Get up to London and away from here for a bit. Then I won't be tempted to meddle. Although I'll feel I'm letting Freda down. She's going to let me know how she gets on with the police. I won't do anything until I hear from her.'

'I'll get on with my writing then,' said John. 'So much easier dealing with murder in fiction. I'm in control and nobody is in control in this real-life case except the murderer.'

And with that dismal thought, he took his leave.

Freda phoned Agatha the next day to say she had told the police and was waiting to hear from them.

Agatha then phoned Roy Silver.

'I was just about to phone you to hear what was happening.'

Agatha gave him all the details, ending up with 'So you see, Roy, I can't really go any further. I was wondering about work.'

'I'll have a word with the boss. But Agatha, sweetie, it's not like you to give up.'

'Oh, really, Sherlock? And what do you suggest?'

'The police have told you time and again in the past to bug out. Did you let it bother you? No. Tell you what. I'll come down at the weekend, bring you another wig and glasses and we'll damn well go round these office girls and see what we can find.'

'I'll get in trouble if we're caught.'

'By the weekend, the police will have interviewed all those office girls to death, and Barrington as well. We've really got to see Zak again. He's the one missing out of all your reports.'

'I'd better not tell John.'

'You mean this writer? He sounds a bit of a stuffed shirt.'

'He's not really. He's just more law-abiding and sensitive than I am.' Agatha regretted her last remark as soon as it was out. She considered herself to be a very sensitive person.

'You mean a bore?'

'No, he's very handsome. Turned out to be not what I thought. But when he's not talking about the case, he is a bit robotic. Never *chats*, you know. See you on Friday evening.'

Agatha put down the phone feeling much better. There was something in John Armitage's character that made her feel, somehow, diminished. She felt the old rebellious Agatha was back. She probably wouldn't see much of John Armitage again. She and the murders had been a diversion.

* * *

To her horror, Roy, descending from the London train on Friday evening, looked like a plucked chicken. He'd had a buzz-cut, which did nothing to enhance his small head and weak features. He was wearing a scarlet shirt with a psychedelic tie under a suede jacket. His thin legs were encased in tight blue jeans and his feet in high-heeled boots.

'Like it?' he said, pirouetting in front of her. 'The latest in the media-chic look.'

'You look like an orphan,' said Agatha.

He put an arm around her. 'You never did move with the times.' He popped on a pair of sun-glasses with wraparound shades. 'There!'

'Oh, God,' said Agatha. 'Never mind.'

John Armitage had just completed the first chapter of his new book and was feeling dissatisfied with it. Somehow Agatha had made him feel that his books were not quite real. He might just pop over to her cottage and discuss it with her.

But as he opened his cottage door, he saw Agatha drive past with a young man in the passenger seat. He retreated indoors. Was that the young man who had stayed with Agatha before and had been described by Mrs Anstruther-Jones as Mrs Raisin's toy-boy? Surely not. But he had not thought of Agatha in any sexual way. He went back to his desk and switched on the computer. He typed in

'Chapter Two' and then stared at the screen. Then he remembered Agatha saying something about asking someone for work. Roy Silver, that was it. So there was nothing to stop him from visiting her.

He switched off the computer and went to Agatha's cottage. Roy answered the door to him.

'I'm John Armitage,' he said.

'And I'm Roy Silver. Agatha's getting changed. We're going out for dinner. Come in.'

John followed him into Agatha's living room. 'Drink?' said Roy. He seemed very much at home.

'Whisky, thanks. Agatha said something about phoning you asking for work.'

'Oh, is that what she told you?'

'Well, yes. What other reason could there be?'

Roy gave him a salacious wink.

'Oh,' said John, feeling discomfited. What on earth could Agatha see in this weird creature?

He took a proffered glass of whisky from Roy. 'Thanks. Known Agatha long?'

'Since I was sixteen. I started work in her business as an office boy. She trained me up to be a public relations officer. I owe her a lot.'

'Did she tell you about this murder we'd been working on?'

'That? Yes, she said something about you wanting to drop the whole thing.'

'Not exactly. There's still a lot to discuss.'

'Maybe some other time.'

Agatha came into the room. She was wearing a soft blouse of swirling colours and a long black skirt slit up the side. John noticed she had excellent legs.

He drained his glass. 'Just called in to say hello. See you again, Agatha.'

He bent down and kissed her cheek. Agatha looked up at him in surprise.

When he had left, she asked Roy, 'Why did he call?'

'Just to say hello. I managed to imply we were having an affair.'

'What on earth did you do that for?'

'I don't know. Maybe a sudden burst of malice. He's very good-looking, but there's something smug about him.'

'I wouldn't call him smug.'

'Anyway, trust me, he will now look at you with new eyes.'

'Roy, he will now find me pathetic.'

Roy had brought Agatha a new wig. The heavy waves of hair hung down on either side of her face, making it look thinner, and the glasses were large, with fake tortoiseshell rims. She tried both on before they left the cottage the following morning. 'Great,' said Roy, surveying the effect. 'Doesn't look like you at all.'

'I'd better take them off now and you can stop somewhere on the road to Evesham and I'll put them on again. If John sees me in the wig, he'll know I've gone back to investigating and he might turn all moral and phone the police.'

Roy looked shocked. 'He wouldn't do that, would he?'

'Maybe not. But I'm not going to risk it.'

On Agatha's instructions, Roy drove into Broadway, instead of taking the bypass.

He pulled into a parking place and waited while Agatha put on the wig and glasses. 'Property values here must have soared after they got the bypass,' said Roy, looking around. 'I remember driving through here when I first came down to see you and the street was jammed with cars and trucks. Are you ready? And who do we try first? We should see Zak.'

'Let's try Sharon Heath first. I'd like to know the repercussions from the attack on Joanna.'

'Talking about Joanna, maybe we should try the hospital later in case she's recovered consciousness.'

'We'll phone first,' said Agatha. 'No point in going all the way to Redditch to find she's still not being allowed visitors.'

Sharon was at home and delighted to see them. They didn't even need to worry about broaching the subject of the attack on Joanna. It was the first thing Sharon wanted to talk about.

'It was ever so odd,' she said when they were seated in the Heaths' cluttered living room. Mrs Heath was not at home, so there had been no hurried cleaning. The remains of a pizza lay on the coffee table surrounded by empty Coke cans and bottles. 'I mean,' Sharon went on, 'she never worked late before. She said she had a couple of accounts to send out. The rest of us left and then I remembered I had left something in my desk.'

'What?' asked Agatha quickly.

'Eh?'

'I mean, what had you forgotten?'

'Oh, er, a scarf. Anyway, I went back for it and she was at her own computer. But she was found at Kylie's computer. The police think she may have been looking for something in the e-mail and they checked out Kylie's computer, but there was no e-mails on it at all. Wiped clean, the policeman said. You should see Mr Barrington these days. Ever such a state he's in. But when the attack took place, he and his missus were at the lawyers. She's asking for a divorce.'

Sharon's eyes gleamed with pleasure at imparting all this delicious gossip.

'Is there any other way into Barrington's, apart from through the front door?' asked Roy.

'Yes, that's where that bastard, George, got into trouble. There's a back door into the workshop and from there you can get along to the offices. The door was unlocked. Mr Barrington was shouting at him something dreadful. George said that he never bothered because he always locked everything up after everyone had gone, and how was he to know someone would creep in and biff Joanna on the head. You never can tell what Joanna's up to. In my opinion, she fancies herself a cut above the rest of us. If she'd told us what she was up to, we'd have stayed with her. So you're still going to do the telly programme?'

'Oh, yes,' lied Agatha. 'But these things take time. As it is all going to be filmed in the disco, we'd better go and see Zak and his father. Will they be at the club now?'

'Might be. They've got to work to clean up the mess from last night. I was there and it was full of people.' She peered at them anxiously. 'You are going to ask me questions about meself? I mean, you're not going to drop everything to do a programme on Kylie's death?'

'Of course not,' said Roy. He made a frame with his hands and looked at Sharon through it. 'Yes, you'll come across well on television.'

Sharon grinned with delight. 'So tell us about your hopes and ambitions,' said Agatha.

'Before you lot came along,' said Sharon, 'I thought I'd meet a nice fellow and have a big wedding and settle down. Maybe two kids. But now I think I'm meant for better things. I mean ter say, the sky's the limit if you put your mind to it.'

Agatha experienced a stab of conscience which she quickly put down to indigestion. Sharon was going on enthusiastically.

'I mean, you know, I always suffered from

174

low self-esteem,' Sharon went on. Agatha reflected that the late Princess Diana had educated the youth of Britain in therapy-speak. 'You know, I'd never have thought I had the looks to go on telly. But it hasn't stopped you getting a job.' She surveyed Agatha.

'I don't appear in front of the cameras,' snapped Agatha.

'You poor old thing. I've got youth on my side.' She turned to Roy. 'What about a bit of plastic surgery? Do you think my nose is too long?'

'No, just right.' They beamed at each other.

'To get back to Kylie,' said Agatha. 'Surely her computer would be checked to see if there were any accounts that needed sending out.'

'Yes, Phyllis was asked to do that, and she ran off any stuff and dealt with it. No one thought about the e-mail.'

'Do you girls often get personal e-mails on your office computers?'

'Ooh, yes. I had this fellow last year who worked in a travel agents and when they weren't looking, he'd send me an e-mail to Barrington's.' She giggled. 'Some of it was pretty hot, so I'd delete it after I'd read it.'

But would Kylie have deleted hers? wondered Agatha. Particularly if there was something she could use as blackmail. Her heart quickened. Or maybe she printed them off and took them home. Perhaps they were still there. But Freda would surely have read them. Still, worth a try. The day had turned warm and the little living room was stifling and permeated with the smell of stale pizza, booze and Sharon's cheap perfume.

'I think that'll be enough for now,' said Agatha, rising to her feet.

'But you'll be back?' asked Sharon.

'Yes, we'll be back.'

'Now what?' asked Roy when they were outside. 'The club?'

'May as well try it.'

But when they got to the club it was closed and locked. 'There's a bell there. Might be someone about.'

'If there isn't, we could call on Freda Stokes,' said Agatha. 'I've been thinking. Maybe Kylie printed off any e-mails in case there was something she could use to blackmail Barrington.'

'Fat chance there's anything at her home,' said Roy. 'I mean, the police will have taken every scrap of paper away and they'll have gone through her belongings.'

'You're right,' said Agatha, downcast. 'Particularly after that business with the bank statements. Ring the bell.'

Roy pressed it and they waited. They were just about to turn away when the door opened. Zak stood there, blinking in the sunlight. He looked as if he had lost weight and there were dark circles under his eyes.

'Oh, you're back,' he said in a lack-lustre way. 'Thought you'd forgotten about us.'

'It all takes ever so much time,' said Roy brightly. 'Just want a few more words.'

'Can't you wait till Dad gets here? He won't be long.'

'It's just a chat,' urged Agatha.

'Okay. Come in.'

He led them through the stale-smelling disco where the staff were busy clearing up, and up to the office. 'Drink?'

'Too early,' said Agatha. She lit up a cigarette. God, it tasted awful. She stubbed it out.

'I'll have one,' said Zak. He poured himself a large glass of vodka and gulped it down, neat.

Roy waited until he had finished and then began questioning him about the disco. How many did they get? Had there ever been any trouble?

Zak slumped down in a chair and answered in a dull voice that they had nearly eighty people on a Saturday night, and, no, they'd never had any trouble – a few scuffles, that was all.

'You must feel you cannot settle to anything, get back to normal, until Kylie's killer is found,' said Agatha.

'If I ever get my hands on the bastard, I'll kill him,' said Zak fiercely. 'She was lovely, my Kylie . . . lovely. And to be snuffed out like that when she was still so young. It don't bear thinking of.' His hands shook and tears spilled down his cheeks. 'The strain of wondering and wondering who did it is wearing me down.'

The office door opened and his father, Terry, came in. His eyes darted from Agatha to Roy and then to his son.

'Look here,' he said truculently, 'Zak's had enough to bear. I don't mind you filming the club, but if you've got any questions about Kylie Stokes, you'd better ask me in future. Go downstairs, Zak, and make sure they're not pinching any booze.'

Zak left. He looked glad to escape.

Agatha was glad of Roy's support. Roy proceeded to question Terry about the club, about the young people, about his life in general, until Agatha could see Terry visibly relax, and even become excited again at the prospect of his club and himself appearing on television.

At last, Roy said he had enough. They were just about to leave when Terry said, 'Wait a minute. Give me your card. If I think of anything, I'll phone you.'

To Agatha's surprise, Roy took out a card case, selected a card and gave it to him. Terry studied it, gave a satisfied grunt, and put it in the pocket of his shirt.

'What number did you give him?' asked Agatha when they were outside on the street.

'My private line at the office. I thought someone would ask us for a card, so I got some printed on one of those machines at the railway station.' He held one out. It said, in neat script, 'Roy Silver, Executive, Pelman Television,' and then the number.

'But what if you're not in your office and the secretary answers?' asked Agatha.

'I primed her. I told her just to say, "Mr Silver's secretary," and then, if someone started asking about television, to field the query.'

'Clever you.'

'Before we try anyone else here, shouldn't we go up to Redditch and see if that girl's regained consciousness?'

'We could phone first. And what if there's a policeman on duty outside her room?'

'So what? We'll say we're relatives.'

Chapter Eight

Agatha was silent on the road to Redditch. Her conscience, never usually very active, was beginning to bother her. She felt responsible for the death of Mrs Anstruther-Jones and for the attack on Joanna. When they were clear of Evesham, she took off the wig and threw it on the back seat and put the glasses in the glove box.

Should there be a policeman on duty outside Joanna's room, then she did not want any report of a woman in a blond wig getting back to headquarters.

'A lot of hospitals don't bother much about visiting hours,' said Roy. 'Let's hope this is one, or that we arrive at the right time.'

'Do we ask at the desk? Or do we just walk in and try to find the right ward?' asked Agatha.

'We'll suss it out when we get there,' he replied.

'Well, well, well,' remarked Roy, as they drove into the car park.

'What?'

'Over there. Just getting out of that BMW. That's John Armitage and carrying a huge bouquet of flowers.'

'Let's join him,' said Agatha.

'No, let's follow him. I bet he knows where to go.'

They scrambled out of the car and set off in pursuit of John. The hospital was busy with visitors arriving and leaving. They followed him along corridors until he stopped at a door and spoke to a policeman sitting outside. The policeman went into the room. Agatha and Roy hid behind a trolley full of laundry. The policeman came out again and said something to John. He went in.

'Let's go,' urged Roy.

Agatha pulled him back. 'We can't.'

'Why not?'

'He'll ask our names. If we give our real names, he'll make a note of it and I might get a rocket from Brudge. If I say I'm Joanna's aunt, she might start screaming that she hasn't got an aunt.'

'Everyone's got an aunt.'

'Her parents are dead. She may not have been in touch with her relatives. No, let's retreat to the car park and question John when he comes out.'

As they stood waiting beside John's car, Roy asked, 'Is he keen on her?'

'Don't be ridiculous. He's old enough to be her grandfather.'

'Makes no difference. That was an awfully big bunch of flowers.'

The inside of Agatha's head felt like a mess. Guilt was swirling around in there, mixed with apprehension, mixed with jealousy that John Armitage, so indifferent to her, should be presenting Joanna with an expensive bunch of flowers.

They waited a full hour before John emerged. 'Come to see Joanna?' he asked, walking up to them.

'We decided it would be better to get a report from you. I'm not a favourite with the police at the moment,' said Agatha. 'And come to think of it, neither are you.'

'Oh, I'm all right. Joanna asked to see me.'

'Why?' demanded Agatha sharply. 'Did she remember anything?'

'Not a thing. The last she knew was a hard blow on the head.'

'This turns out to have been one wasted journey. What about going back to Evesham, Agatha sweetie, and question some of the others?' said Roy.

'She can't do that,' said John. 'She'd need to wear her disguise, and apart from the fact that the police have got it, she's been warned off.'

'I'll sit in the car and let Roy do the questioning,' said Agatha quickly. 'You were in there for an hour. What did you talk about?'

'Books, films, things like that.'

'Come along, Roy. You can drive.' Agatha

turned on her heel and headed for her own car without so much as a goodbye.

John followed them down the road to Evesham. He noticed, as they were approaching the town, that Agatha leaned over to the back seat and picked up a blond wig and began to arrange it on her head. What on earth was she doing, keeping up the masquerade when the police had told her not to?

But he felt he was being left out. Could Agatha really be having an affair with that young fellow? Roy had implied as much. Roy would need to leave for work on Sunday evening. Better leave things until then and call on Agatha.

'Who next?' asked Roy.

'I don't know,' said Agatha wearily. She suddenly just wanted to go home and forget there was the real world out there, where handsome men, however old, preferred pretty young girls.

'Buck up, Aggie. You can't win them all.'

'It's your fault. You should never have let him think we were having an affair.'

'If it makes you feel better to think that . . . Anyway, turn your mind to the problem at hand. Who have we got?'

'I think,' said Agatha reluctantly, 'that the best person to see next is the horrible Phyllis. She hated Kylie. Kylie took her boyfriend away. She might let something slip.'

'Got her phone number?'

Agatha leaned over to the back seat and picked up a clipboard. 'I've got all the phone numbers and addresses here.'

'So let's phone her. Ask her to meet us. Where?'

'There's a good pub round the corner from the car park. Pub grub.'

'That'll do. So phone her.'

'You do it. I can't stand her and I need a little more time to psych myself up.'

Roy phoned Phyllis's number. Agatha's thoughts drifted back to John as she dimly heard Roy making arrangements for lunch. He seemed such an *asexual* man. Could he really be interested in Joanna? And had his ex-wife really been such a monster or was there something wrong with him?

She jerked away from her thoughts as Roy said, 'Come on. Stop dreaming about what might have been. Let's go and meet Phyllis.'

Although the pub was only a short walk from Phyllis's flat, it was a good half-hour before she arrived. Agatha, on seeing her, judged that Phyllis must have taken the time to plaster on an extra layer of make-up. Her fleshy features were covered in a thick white foundation cream and blusher. Her eyelashes had so much mascara on them that they stuck out like wires and her lips, already large, had been made larger by a coat of scarlet lipstick.

When she had ordered her food and drink, Roy said, 'I think you're ever so brave.'

'Why's that?' said Phyllis. She moistened her lips and wondered what her chances were of fascinating this television executive.

'I mean, you're still working at Barrington's. You must be wondering if you'll be next.'

'Not me,' said Phyllis. 'Let me give you the low-down on our little Kylie. She was a nasty little bitch, batting her eyes at anything in trousers. And screwing around with the boss.'

'How did you learn that?' asked Agatha.

Phyllis looked mysterious. 'Little bird.'

'But who would kill her?' asked Roy.

Phyllis leaned forward until her bust was resting on the table. 'Shershy loam,' she said.

'What?' Agatha looked at her, puzzled.

Phyllis gave a superior laugh. 'It means "Look for the man."'

'You mean, *cherchez l'homme*?'

'That's what I said, didn't I? Anyway, with a tart like Kylie, there's bound to have been more than one Mr Barrington.'

'Anyone you can think of?'

'Naw, but the police'll find him. She got what was coming to her.'

'You're an intelligent girl and you've certainly given us something to think about,' said Roy.

Phyllis tried to bat her eyelashes at him, but the wiry upper set got stuck to the lower ones and so there was a silence until she had prised them apart.

'What about the evening Joanna was attacked?' asked Agatha. 'Sharon said she went back for a scarf. Did she join you again? And did she have a scarf?'

'Didn't notice.' Phyllis held up her empty glass. 'Another of these? I mean, you're on expenses anyway.

Roy went to the bar to get more drinks.

'Nice bum,' said Phyllis, surveying Roy's back.

Agatha reflected that as Roy was so skinny and his jacket hung down over his rear, Phyllis was not in a position to judge. Phyllis was possibly just aping what the women's magazines told her to say. Did women really admire men's bottoms? Or had it started as a sort of feminist remark to try to even the sexes?

Roy came back. 'Thanks. Cheers,' said Phyllis. 'Where was I? Oh, Joanna. That's a dark horse. Little Miss Prim. She's involved somehow. Must have been worried there was something on Kylie's computer that might incriminate her. Here's a thing!' Her eyes gleamed. 'Harry McCoy, he told me that one evening, he saw Barrington driving past him on Evesham High Street and he could have sworn that Joanna was in the car next to him.'

I hope that's true and I wonder what John will make of it, thought Agatha. I'm a bit tired of Saint Joanna.

Their food arrived. Agatha stared at Phyllis in amazement. She had never seen anyone eat so quickly. One minute her large mouth was bent down over the plate, and it seemed as if the next minute the plate was empty. Like watching a vacuum cleaner sucking up food.

Phyllis then went on to describe her hopes of becoming a television star. She pointed out that she was the only one of the girls with any looks to qualify for stardom.

Agatha and Roy ate steadily and tried not to listen as Phyllis's harsh voice went on and on. They would have liked to escape, but Phyllis demanded more drink and pudding and so they had to wait until she had demolished a large helping of apple pie and custard washed down with a double vodka and Red Bull. Her face flushed with drink and food, she went on and on until at last they were able to make their escape.

'Phew!' said Roy when they were free of her. 'Now what?'

'I can't bear listening to any more of these silly girls' dreams of stardom,' said Agatha. 'Let's ask John if he can find out from Joanna about Barrington.'

'Harry McCoy could have been mistaken. And you're jealous of John's interest in this Joanna.'

'I am not! It's too good a lead to ignore.'

John was at home when they arrived. He listened to them carefully and then said, 'He was probably just giving her a lift home.'

'Along the High Street?' jeered Agatha. 'Wrong way.'

'Well, I suppose I've got nothing better to do.

I'll run back up to Redditch and let you know what she says.'

'What about a visit to your friend, Mrs Bloxby?' suggested Roy when John had driven off. 'We'll tell her what we've got and see what she says. She's very intelligent.'

'She may be busy,' protested Agatha, who did not like hearing something that suggested Mrs Bloxby might have better powers of deduction than she had herself.

'We can try.'

Mrs Bloxby was at home and pleased to see them. Agatha rather sulkily listened as Roy outlined the latest findings.

'It must have something to do with drugs,' said Mrs Bloxby.

'Why?' demanded Agatha. 'I think it's got something to do with blackmail and jealousy.'

'Just a feeling. Say someone knew about how worried Kylie was about that wedding dress. And that someone phones her up, or if it was one of those office girls, says to her something like "Why don't you nip out of the house with it and let me have a look?" Kylie had probably drunk a lot at the hen party and so she wouldn't see anything odd in going out in the middle of the night with it.'

'Surely the police have thought of that. They must be looking for someone who saw a girl carrying a dress through the streets of Evesham at night.'

Agatha lit up a cigarette, made a face and stubbed it out again. Why had she even tried? And she had never lit up a cigarette in the rectory before.

'To turn to parish matters,' said Mrs Bloxby. 'We have a gentleman who is mounting an exhibition of old photographs of the Cotswolds in the school hall a week on Friday. Admission to the exhibition is only twenty pee. But to raise some extra money, we are having teas and cakes. May I rely on your support, Mrs Raisin?'

'No use asking her,' crowed Roy. 'She can't bake.'

Agatha scowled horribly.

'I meant, could you help with serving the teas? Mrs Anstruther-Jones was one of our helpers, and the poor woman can't do it now.'

Guilt over Mrs Anstruther-Jones's death prompted Agatha to say gruffly, 'Yes, put me down.'

'Splendid.'

I wonder how John's getting on, thought Agatha.

John entered Joanna's hospital room quietly. She was lying asleep and looked very young and fragile. He put the box of chocolates he had brought her on the table beside the bed. Joanna's eyes opened and she looked up at him.

'John!' she exclaimed, a delicate pink colouring her cheeks. 'Two visits in one day. I've got good news, too. I'm to go home tomorrow.'

'They're sure?'

'Yes, I'm completely recovered.' She eased herself up against the pillows and gave him a radiant smile.

'Joanna, there's one little thing that made me curious. It's about the Kylie Stokes business.'

Her eyes flirted with him. 'And I thought you came rushing back to see me.'

'It's just that you were seen one evening in Barrington's car going along Evesham High Street.'

'He gave me a lift home one evening.' She looked down and plucked at the bedcovers. He noticed she had painted her nails red, and Joanna wasn't what he would have considered a red-nails sort of person. Oh, really? jeered Agatha Raisin's voice in his head. And just what is a red-nails sort of person?

'Joanna,' he persisted, 'if he had been driving you home, he wouldn't have gone by way of the High Street.'

There was a long silence. Then she asked in a small voice, 'Will you be telling the police?'

'Agatha and I are not particularly popular with the police at the moment. But I think you'd better tell me about it.'

'He's not a very nice person,' mumbled Joanna.

'I know that. I gathered that.' He took a deep breath. 'Did you have an affair with him?'

She blushed as red as her nails.

'Yes,' she whispered.

John had a sudden mental picture of Barrington with his florid face, thinning hair, and hairy hands. 'Why, in God's name?'

'It started when he did give me a run home one night and he did go home first to pick up some files. He said there was a new restaurant just opened up in Cirencester, very expensive, and perhaps I would like to go? I'd never been to an expensive restaurant before and I thought it would be a bit of fun. I enjoyed myself. He told me he was planning to get a divorce. He'd made a mistake in his marriage. He said the business was doing well and he could soon afford to take a holiday – maybe the Caribbean – and he wished he could take someone like me. I've never been abroad. I'm ambitious. I want to see the world. I thought, why not? He said if I'd go with him, he'd get a divorce and marry me, so it wasn't as if I would be committing adultery or anything.

'We started to have an affair. I suppose it wasn't what you'd call an affair. Three evenings at my place, that was all. I didn't enjoy it a bit, but I thought what marriage to him would entail. Being able to go to posh places and glamorous holidays. Then he just stopped seeing me. After a week, I went into his office. He blustered and said he'd been busy. The business wasn't doing as well as he'd thought and his wife had invested in it. I felt such a fool. But I hadn't been in love with him so it wasn't that bad until I found he'd been going out with Kylie. So I took it upon myself to warn her off. She just laughed at me and told me to go and take a good look in the mirror. Barrington may not have been serious about someone like me, she said, but he was dead serious about her. I hated her. Silly little bitch.'

John felt sad. Joanna thought she was a cut above the rest of them and he had believed that, too. She had read and admired his books, so, with his writer's vanity, he had assumed she must be intelligent.

'Did you kill Kylie?' he asked.

'Of course not. What do you take me for? She wasn't worth the effort.'

Joanna lay back on the pillows and closed her eyes.

'I'd better be going,' said John.

Joanna's eyes flew open. 'But I'll see you soon. We'll go to that restaurant again and have a chat.'

'I'm going to be very busy,' said John. 'New book to write. I won't be socializing for a while.'

She studied him, her eyes suddenly hard. 'The police don't know it was you who put me up to searching Kylie's e-mail. Maybe I'll tell them.'

'Then you'll only look very silly for not having told them in the first place. They will call on me and I will be obliged to tell them what you've just told me about Barrington.'

John turned on his heel and walked out.

* * *

As he drove back, he could feel a great loathing about telling Agatha Joanna's story welling up in him. It is a sad fact that there are no new wounds, only old wounds reopened, and the distasteful incident with Joanna had only served to remind him of the failure of his marriage. His wife had been so very beautiful and he so proud of her. Speaking at writers' conferences, he had enjoyed a thrill every time at looking down from the podium and seeing her blond beauty staring rapturously up at him. When he had found out about her first affair, he had been devastated. She had wept and promised that it would never happen again. But it had, several times, until the humiliation he had felt had killed love. Not that he had loved Joanna or had planned to take the friendship any further. But he had been flattered by the way she had hung on his every word. In fact, he remembered now that, over dinner, it had been he who had talked of books and plays and films while Joanna had breathlessly agreed with everything he had said.

He decided to drive straight on to London and spend some time with friends. But if he didn't return home to the village, Agatha would phone the police. And he needed to pack.

He didn't need to tell Agatha about Barrington and Joanna. Surely that had nothing to do with the case. Anyway, he should have left the whole thing to the police.

* * *

'There was something odd there,' said Agatha to Roy, after John had explained that Joanna had claimed that Barrington had been giving her a lift home but calling at his home first to pick up some files.

'Yes,' agreed Roy. 'He looked more wooden-faced than ever. Doesn't ever give much away, does he? And he's shooting off to London.'

'There was something at the back of his eyes,' said Agatha. 'He looked hurt. I bet the silly fool made a pass at her and got rejected. Clown!'

'Too right,' cackled Roy. 'Why couldn't he have made a pass at you, eh?'

'I'm weary,' said Agatha, ignoring the gibe. 'I don't want to ask any more questions.'

'Not even to find out what he really said to Joanna? Come on, Aggie. Curiosity's killing me and he said she was being released tomorrow. Wouldn't do any harm to drop in on her. I mean, do you really believe that stuff about Barrington going home first to pick up some files? Why not drop Joanna off first?'

'All right,' said Agatha. 'May as well try her.' And if, she thought privately, John Armitage did make a pass at someone as young as she is, then I needn't bother with him again.

Joanna answered the door to them next day looking bright and fresh and pretty, as if she had not recently gone through such an ordeal. But her face fell when she saw Agatha and she peered round her. Looking for John, thought Agatha. 'This is a friend of mine, Roy Silver,' said Agatha, introducing him. 'May we come in?'

'Yes, of course. Where's John?'

'Gone to London.'

She gave a little shrug and walked ahead of them into the living room.

'So,' began Agatha, settling herself on a sofa next to Roy, 'can you remember anything at all about the attack?'

'Not a thing,' said Joanna. 'One minute I was sitting in front of Kylie's computer, and then the next, I was struck on the head and that's the last I remember until I came to in hospital.'

Agatha decided to pretend that John had not told them anything. 'I heard that you were seen one evening in Barrington's car, going along the High Street.'

Joanna rose to her feet and took some dead flowers out of a vase and put them in the garbage bin. She returned and at down. 'Sorry. Just tidying up. You were saying?'

Agatha repeated it. 'John asked me about that,' said Joanna. 'What did he tell you?'

'He didn't tell us anything,' said Agatha.

'It was simply that Mr Barrington had to collect some files from home before going on to Birmingham. He said he would pick them up and then run me home.'

'Was this unexpected?' asked Agatha. 'I mean, had he offered to run you home before?'

'Never.'

'So why this time?'

'Why, why, why?' demanded Joanna angrily. 'I happened to be leaving as he was leaving. That's all.'

Joanna's faced was flushed and she was staring at the floor.

'No, I don't think that's all,' said Agatha. 'We're not the police. Why don't you get it off your chest?'

Joanna glared at her. 'That rat told you.'

Identifying the rat as John, Agatha smiled enigmatically.

'So it was a brief fling until he dumped me for Kylie,' Joanna spat out.

'You must have hated her.'

'She was a grasping silly bitch.'

'A blackmailing silly bitch, too,' said Agatha. 'You didn't try to blackmail him yourself?'

'What do you take me for?'

'I don't know. I wouldn't in a million years have supposed you would have an affair with a man like Barrington.'

'He promised to marry me. He said he would take me on holiday. It's all right for a rich old cow like you –'

'Watch your mouth!'

'Anyway,' said Joanna sulkily, 'you don't know what it's like never to have travelled, never to be able to afford to go to good restaurants, buying clothes in thrift shops. These old men are all the same. I hate old people.' Her eyes suddenly lit up with malice.

'John Armitage was another one. He wanted

me to move in with him. Can you believe it? But I knew he would turn out like Barrington, so I turned him down. It's no use asking him about it; he'll deny it.'

'I'm sure he will,' said Roy. 'Do you think Barrington was involved in any way with Kylie's death? He may not have done it himself but he could have paid someone to do it.'

'He probably did. I wouldn't put anything past him.'

'I don't think so,' interrupted Roy. 'I mean, he had paid her the hush money and it was in her account.'

'She could have asked for more.'

'I think that will be all for the moment.' Agatha stood up.

'I think that'll be all forever,' said Joanna. 'Get out and don't come back.'

'Wow,' said Roy as they retreated to the nearest pub. 'What did you think of all that? I don't think for a moment that Armitage made a pass at her.'

'Oh, really? Then why didn't he tell us?'

'Probably did fancy her and felt like a fool when he found out she was just a little gold-digger. I must say, they all seem a horrible bunch of girls.'

'The Russians have a saying: The fish always rots from the head down. You have a rotten boss and you get rotten staff.'

'Do you think, Agatha, that the business is really successful? There's all that about his wife having the money.'

'I'm weary.'

'We shouldn't give up. Are there any of these girls that seem decent and ordinary to you?'

'There's Ann Trump. Lives with her parents. Seems straightforward enough.'

'Let's try her.'

Once they were both seated facing Ann Trump some ten minutes later, Agatha, once more wearing her disguise, began to wonder how to broach the subject of Kylie Stokes and Joanna Field. Ann was so obviously thrilled to be receiving yet another visit from the 'television people'.

At last, after Agatha had pretended to take copious notes on Ann's life, she said, 'How do you get on with the other girls in the office?'

'Oh, we rub along, you know.'

'You must all be feeling afraid after what happened to Joanna.'

'Yes, isn't it scary? But, I mean, whoever attacked her won't try again. And she was evidently checking Kylie's e-mail.'

'I want to ask you a personal question. Did your boss ever come on to you?'

Her eyes widened in surprise. 'You mean, Mr Barrington? No, he didn't. Until I heard about him and Kylie, I'd never have thought he'd do anything like that.'

Agatha hesitated. Did she owe Joanna any loyalty? No. 'Did you know that he also had an affair, a very brief affair, with Joanna?'

'Why, that dirty old man! And Joanna! Always a bit prim and proper. I mean, she'd always come along for a drink with us, if one of us had a birthday. But she'd never really join in. She'd always be the first to leave the pub.'

'What about the night of the hen party?'

'She stayed to the end, until we all walked into Evesham and split up. Phyllis wasn't there but then she had it in for Kylie because of Zak. Hey, do you think it might have been Phyllis who struck Joanna?'

'Why would she do that?'

'I dunno. I begin to think I don't know anything. I mean, if Mr Barrington hit on Joanna and Kylie, he might have tried it on with Phyllis. Wait till I see Joanna when she gets back to work. I'll take her down a peg or two.'

Agatha said uneasily, 'Please don't do that. Do treat what we say to you in the utmost confidence. If you are going to be on television, it is essential that you know how to be discreet.'

'I won't breathe a word.' Ann's eyes shone at the thought of being on television. Again Agatha felt that stab of conscience.

'Didn't get anything out of that,' remarked Roy, after they had left.

'I really want to drop the whole thing,' said

Agatha. 'I hope she doesn't tell Joanna anything.'

'Why?'

'I'm afraid of Joanna. She knows my real identity and she knows where I live.'

'Were you as taken in by her as John obviously was?'

'Yes, I really did think she was a cut above the other girls. She certainly fooled me. I think we'd better call on Freda Stokes. She might know if the police have found out anything.'

Freda was at home and pleased to see them. She listened carefully as Agatha told her everything they had found out.

'The police don't know about Joanna and Barrington. Should I tell them?' asked Freda.

'Not at the moment because they would want to know how you found out and that would land us in trouble. Have they told you what lines they are working on?'

'No. They came back again and searched her room. They'd already taken a lot of stuff away.'

'Like what?'

'Aspirin bottles, cosmetics, stuff like that. They were looking for any trace of drugs. They even took her dolls and stuffed animals.'

'No point in us looking, then,' said Agatha. 'Did Kylie ever say anything about Joanna?'

'I can't remember. It was usually Phyllis she was complaining about.'

'Did she have one particular friend amongst the girls? She took that wedding gown to show someone.'

'She never seemed to have any of them round the house. Harry McCoy might know.'

Agatha took out her mobile phone. 'May as well have another chat to him.' She checked her clipboard and dialled his number. Roy heard her say, 'Harry? We're still going ahead with the television programme and wanted to ask you some more questions. Can we meet you at that café where we met before? Good. About fifteen minutes.'

Agatha rang off. 'May as well keep trying,' she said.

If only, thought Agatha, I could drop this masquerade of being with a television company and cut to the chase instead of pretending to be interested in this young man's supremely uninteresting social life. But she patiently took notes and then finally asked him, 'What did you think of the attack on Joanna Field?'

'I don't know what to make of it,' said Harry. 'I mean, she was at Kylie's computer and someone obviously didn't want her to read what was on there.'

Agatha wondered whether to tell him about Joanna, but dreaded Phyllis's reaction. And yet, why protect Joanna? But she asked, 'Kylie, we think, was worried about her wedding gown. We think she wanted to show it to someone. Was she particularly close to any of the girls?'

'She didn't seem to be. She would laugh

about them, you know, call Joanna stuck-up, and Phyllis ugly, and say she wasn't going to be tied down doing accounts and sales for a plumbing firm. I know they all occasionally got together for a drink. That's all. I mean, it would need to be someone pretty special to get her out in the middle of the night. What about Zak?'

'I don't think she'd want him to see it before the wedding,' said Agatha.

'Have you seen Joanna?' asked Harry.

'Yes, she's out of hospital and is fully recovered.'

'And did she actually see anything on Kylie's computer?'

'No, she says she switched it on and then someone hit her on the head.'

'Will all this stuff on Kylie's death be on telly?'

Roy spoke for the first time. 'We're doing some background on it because we can hardly do a programme on the youth of Evesham without mentioning her death. It's been in all the papers.'

Harry laughed. 'Phyllis won't like that. Being upstaged by Kylie even when she's dead.'

Agatha looked at his laughing face. 'Didn't you mourn Kylie's death?'

'What? Well, of course. In a way. I mean, when she died, it wasn't as if she was my girl any more.'

'But you had been intimate with her.'

'Not for a bit, though.'

He never really knew Kylie, thought Agatha. He had found her decorative and that had been enough.

Agatha saw Roy off at the station that evening. After Harry, they had decided not to see anyone else. They had returned to Agatha's cottage and had typed out what they had discovered and it seemed to lead absolutely nowhere.

After playing with her cats, Agatha went up to bed, feeling suddenly lonely. She showered and got ready for bed. She tried to read a light romance, but the words could not take her mind off the case. There was one little thing. One dangerous little thing she had missed.

Then she sat bolt upright. Had Joanna found anything among the e-mails on Kylie's machine before someone hit her? And if she did, would she be stupid enough to try to use it to blackmail the murderer? If Joanna could have an affair with a man like Barrington and all because of money, would she not see incriminating evidence against someone as a golden opportunity to get out of the rut?

Agatha got out of bed and began to pace up and down. There must be some way of letting the police know that Joanna had been involved with Barrington. The silly girl's life could be in danger. If she phoned, her voice might be recognized and she was hopeless at imitating accents. Then she thought, there was one accent, no longer hers, buried deep down inside her under layers of Mayfair – that of the Birmingham slums.

She went downstairs, picked up the phone and was about to dial Worcester police when she remembered the call could be traced. She pulled a long coat on over her nightgown, drew on a pair of thin gloves, and went out and got into her car. She drove steadily through the dark to Evesham and to the station. She went to the public phone outside and dialled Worcester police. 'Listen 'ere,' she said gruffly when a policewoman answered. 'That Kylie Stokes murder. Joanna Field, her that was hit on the 'ead, was having an affair with Barrington. She saw somethink on that e-mail and is going to blackmail someone.'

'Who is this?' demanded the voice sharply.

Agatha dropped the phone, got into her car, and drove off out by the ring road, knowing the police would trace the call to the phone box and send someone there as fast as possible. Her heart lurched as she remembered seeing a forensic-science programme which said they would soon be able to tell who had used a phone by their DNA. Anyone using a phone left a certain amount of their DNA on the receiver. How old had that programme been? Could they do it now? Then her hands relaxed on the steering wheel. Her fingerprints were on record from previous cases but not her DNA and they had no reason to ask for a sample.

She felt sleepy by the time she arrived back home, relaxed now with the comfortable feeling that she had done her best.

In the following days, Agatha put the case of Kylie Stokes out of her mind. It was suddenly a great relief to let go of it. She felt slightly guilty when she thought of Freda Stokes, but assured herself that she had done all that she could do. John Armitage was still in London. She would follow his example and leave well enough alone.

But by the end of the week, she concluded it would be only decent to go and see Freda Stokes and tell her what she had decided.

Accordingly she went to Evesham Market to where Freda was working at her stall. 'Don't say anything here,' said Freda. She called to a woman at the stall opposite. 'Could you mind things for me, Gladys? Going for a cuppa.'

'Sure,' said Gladys. 'Quiet as the grave today.'

They went to a café at the back of the covered market. Agatha ordered two cups of tea and carried them to a table. Freda's first words appalled her. 'I suppose you're worried about Joanna.'

'What about Joanna?' Agatha's heart gave a lurch.

'She's missing. I had the police round. She hadn't been at work, but that wasn't why they were worried. They had a mysterious call from someone telling them that Joanna'd had an affair with Barrington and was going to blackmail someone. They kept calling at her flat and when they didn't get a reply, they finally broke in. No sign of her. No note. No clothes had been packed. Nothing missing. Except Joanna.'

Too late, thought Agatha. I was too late.

'It's like a nightmare,' said Freda. 'Some murderer's prowling about. Why can't the police do anything?'

Maybe because I kept the information to myself for just that bit too long, thought Agatha sadly.

'I'm not much of a help, Freda,' she said. 'I've been trying and trying and all I do is dig up more muck without ever finding out who did the murder.'

'If we never know,' said Freda miserably, 'I can never feel that my poor girl is resting easy in her grave.'

'Have they released the body for burial?'

'Yes, the funeral's tomorrow. We're keeping it quiet. Don't want the press around.'

'Where is the funeral to take place?'

'At Saint Edmund's up on Greenhill at eleven in the morning. Will you come?'

'Yes, I'll be there.'

The funeral of Kylie Stokes took place on a warm sunny Saturday. Zak was there with his father and the girls from the office, minus Joanna. The service was brief and simple.

Freda was red-eyed but tearless, as if she had shed so many tears over her daughter's death that there were none left. Zak was supported by his father. He had lost more weight and was white-faced with grief. Agatha was wearing a large hat and dark glasses in case any of the office girls should recognize her without her disguise. She wished she had not come.

Kylie might not have been the angel her mother had once believed her to be, but she had been so young and pretty – too young and pretty to lie so soon in the warm earth on a sunny day.

I must find out who did it, thought Agatha. But how?

Chapter Nine

When Agatha returned home, she sat down at her computer to go through her notes. She managed to catch Boswell in mid-air as he was about to leap on the keyboard. She carried the protesting cat out to the garden, followed by Hodge. 'Stay there,' she ordered. They both sat side by side on the lawn, staring at her, as if she had committed some outrage. Agatha shut the door on them and returned to the computer.

She printed out what she had written and retreated to the kitchen with the pile of papers. Agatha made a cup of black coffee and lit a cigarette. She sighed. It still tasted like burning rubber. She left it burning in the ashtray but a smell, like smouldering tyres on a used-tyre dump, began to fill the kitchen. She sighed again and stubbed it out. She opened the kitchen door to clear the air. 'You can come in now,' she said to her cats. They turned their backs on her and strolled off down the garden.

Agatha shrugged and retreated to her notes. Now, was there anything she had missed?

There was something Mary Webster had said. Where was it? At last she had it. Mary Webster had said that she had caught Kylie in the ladies' room smoking pot. Now, as pot was still an illegal substance, anyone who wanted it had to go to an illegal source and illegal sources often pushed harder drugs. Why had she, Agatha, let this one slide by? Then there was one other thing nagging at her brain.

She closed her eyes and remembered looking down from the bridge at the flood, seeing Kylie floating underneath, her hair swirling in the water, the white wedding dress, like a shroud, the bouquet clutched in stiff hands. Her eyes snapped open. The bouquet! Yes, she could have gone to show someone the wedding gown. But the bouquet! She glanced at the clock. Freda would be at home. She had surely taken the day off for the funeral.

Agatha phoned Freda and when she got her on the line, she asked, 'Freda, Kylie was clutching a wedding bouquet when she was found. How did she get it? Did you keep it at home?'

'No, the police asked me that. I'd ordered it from that florists next to the market. It was to be of red roses and lilies and some maidenhair fern. It hadn't been collected. It hadn't even been made. They were sending it round on the morning of the wedding day.'

'And that was Kylie's choice?'

'Well, no. She'd left all the wedding arrangements to me and Terry. Terry was paying for the wedding, but I was paying for the wedding gown and the bouquet and the bridesmaids' dresses.'

'Who were the bridesmaids? Anyone from the office?'

'No, Iris was going to be one bridesmaid, and my brother Frank's girl, Ruby, the other. And then Iris's little daughter, Haley, was going to be flower-girl.'

'Did Kylie object to the bouquet as much as she objected to the wedding gown?'

'Well, she did. She said she wanted white roses.'

'Did the police say anything about what the bouquet was like?'

'No, it was never found. It must have come loose from her hands. They said with so much debris and so much of the floodwater pouring into people's homes and shops and basements, it could be anywhere.'

Agatha thought furiously. The drowned Kylie had been clutching that bouquet. Hard to tell with the swirling of the water what it had been like. Agatha was sure that bouquet had contained white roses.

'Do you know if Kylie told anyone about the fact that she didn't like the bouquet you had chosen for her?'

'She was angry about it and the dress. I usually gave in to her, but not on this. As I told you, I couldn't afford a new gown for her, and I didn't see any reason to. Iris's gown was beautiful and as good as new. I could have changed the order for the flowers, but to tell the truth, I was so mad because Kylie had taken no interest in the wedding preparations, I dug my heels in and said I'd no intention of changing anything at all.' Freda began to sob. 'If only she were alive, she could have anything sh-she w-wanted.'

Agatha tried to comfort her but Freda said she was too upset to talk any longer. Agatha said goodbye and then sat biting her nails, a substitute for nicotine. Those flowers. Now if they had been in the deep freeze with Kylie's body, they would be frost-blasted and black. So someone must have put the bouquet in the dead girl's cold frozen hands before putting her in the river. She shuddered. There was something very evil about that macabre touch of the bouquet. It had been done with hate.

She longed to phone Freda again and ask if she told the police about the row over the bouquet. Had the police checked all the florists to see if anyone had ordered a bouquet of white roses?

Then she thought, why not phone the police? She had not found out about the bouquet by any questioning in disguise. She telephoned Worcester police and was put through to Brudge. He listened to her carefully and then said, 'There were little marks on her hands as if from thorns. Thank you, Mrs Raisin; we'll look into it.'

Agatha put down the phone with a feeling of relief. The police had the resources to cover florists far and wide.

She went back to her notes. Kylie must have been close to one of the girls. Just suppose one of them suggested to her at the hen party that she should slip out after she got home and bring the dress with her? She sat back and frowned. Wedding presents. She had never asked about the wedding presents. Now if one of the girls had given a particularly expensive wedding present, would that not go to show particular friendship?

Agatha was reluctant to phone Freda again, but curiosity compelled her to dial her number.

'I don't want to upset you further,' said Agatha. 'What about the wedding presents?'

'I returned them all,' said Freda in a tired voice.

'Can you by any chance remember what the office girls gave her?'

'It was a joint present, a tea-service.'

'Nothing else?'

'I made a list. I may still have it. Hold on.'

Agatha waited impatiently. Freda came back on the line. 'I've found it. Oh, Joanna Field – poor Joanna, the police haven't found her – gave her a bottle of perfume as well as contributing to the tea-service. And Marilyn Josh gave her one of those indecent thong swimsuits. I remember Kylie saying, "She must think I'm a tart." Nothing else.'

After she had rung off, Agatha studied the notes of Marilyn Josh. Marilyn lived above Harry McCoy and could have seen Agatha standing outside the house that evening when someone had tried to run her over. But Marilyn would not have the means to inject Kylie with heroin and then dump her body in a freezer. Unless she had help. Or had Joanna been in on it and had she disappeared to somewhere she was sure the police would not find her?

The doorbell rang. Agatha opened the door to find Mrs Bloxby there. 'You haven't forgotten about the old photographs of the Cotswolds thing?' she asked anxiously.

'I had,' said Agatha ruefully.

'It's tomorrow at three in the afternoon. All you have to do is serve tea, sandwiches and cakes.'

'Oh, all right. I'll be there. Lantern-slides?'

'No, framed photographs around the walls. Easy, pleasant afternoon.'

'For some,' muttered Agatha. 'Come in. I'll make some coffee.'

'I have to get on. Is John Armitage back? His car isn't there.'

'I neither know nor care,' said Agatha stiffly.

'Oh, *Mrs Raisin!*'

'Mrs Raisin what?' But the vicar's wife was walking rapidly away.

Agatha decided to check her e-mail. There was one from Marie Hernandez. 'We are going back to Robinson Crusoe Island in August and wondered if you would like to join us? We had such fun and I think it was a healing place for you. Let us know if you'll be there.'

Agatha thought of the long, long plane flight to Santiago and then the three-hour flight in the small propeller plane out to the island. She typed, 'I don't think I can make it. Maybe next year.' She hesitated. Should she tell Marie about the case she was on? But it was too complicated and would take too long. So she added a few sentences about the weather in true British style and sent it off.

The doorbell rang again. It was Bill Wong. Agatha eagerly drew him in and described how she had phoned Brudge about the flowers.

'Good work,' said Bill. 'I heard a while back from my friend at Worcester police that they had been asking about that bouquet, but the people with you on the bridge when Kylie was spotted were too shocked to notice if the bouquet was fresh. Anything else?'

'Did I tell you that Mary Webster once caught Kylie smoking pot?'

'No, I don't think you did. That's interesting. If she was experimenting with pot, she might have gone on to experiment with something stronger. Did she tell Mary where she'd got it?'

'No. Well, I forgot to ask that.'

'And I hear from the news that Joanna Field is still missing.'

'I wonder, Bill, if she had anything to do with it. I wonder if she thought the police might soon get on to her and decided to disappear.'

'I almost wish that were the case. But would she go off and not take any of her clothes with her? She has only a little bit of money in her account and none of it has been touched. How's John Armitage?'

Agatha stared at him. 'There's a thing. I wonder.'

'What?'

'He was keen on her. He found out she'd been sleeping with Barrington – what a euphemism, sleeping. Anyway, he took off after that. But he *was* keen on her. What if she gave him some sob story about wanting to get away from it all?'

'I think you'll probably find that John Armitage left news of his whereabouts with Worcester police before he left. But I'll phone them and check him out. You know, it's a pity it wasn't Zak. It's usually the nearest and dearest.'

'But he's so cut up. And what could his motive be?'

'If there were drugs at that club and Kylie

had somehow found out and threatened to tell the police, that would be a motive. But the club's been searched. And there's never been a whisper of anything there. It could be jealousy on the part of one of the girls. But would any of them go to such lengths? Trying to kill you and then succeeding in running down Mrs Anstruther-Jones?'

Agatha lit a cigarette, took a puff, winced and put it out. 'I don't know, Bill. I just don't know.'

He smiled. 'Relax, Agatha. You've done your best. The police will be combing the florists far and wide. That was a good tip. Leave everything to them.'

Agatha retreated to the garden to start weeding again. The weather had turned very warm and heavy. She noticed that the grass on the lawn had grown several inches. Again she thought of calling the gardener, but stopped herself from doing so with the reminder that she might as well occupy her time, and why pay someone to do what she could do herself?

She got the lawn-mower out of the shed at the foot of the garden, carried the lead into the kitchen and plugged it in.

Back in the garden, she switched on the machine and began to trundle it happily up and down the grass in the sunshine, dreaming of becoming a completely new Agatha Raisin, in the way that people who do not like themselves very much are apt to do when they set about inventing a new character for themselves. She would take lessons in cookery and baking from Mrs Bloxby. She would become a model villager. She would fund-raise for the church. Her thoughts began to take a gloomy turn. Yes, she would be the perfect country lady, and at her funeral the church would be filled with sobbing villagers. Alf, the vicar, would be in tears as he explained to the packed congregation that he really did not know how he or the village would get along without her. Perhaps James Lacey would be there, head bowed by her graveside. He would say, 'I loved her all my life and came back to tell her so, but it was too late.' A tear rolled down Agatha's cheek and she brushed it angrily away.

The grass done and the cut grass bagged up in refuse sacks, Agatha went back indoors and decided to do a particularly tough Pilates exercise called the dead bug, which involved lying on her back and stretching alternate legs and arms until she ached.

What next? A shopping trip? But where? Stow-on-the-Wold and Chipping Campden were wall-to-wall tourists. Much as she liked Evesham, it didn't have much in the way of smart clothes shops.

The doorbell shrilled. Glad of a diversion, Agatha hurried to open it and then glared at

Sir Charles Fraith. Certainly, he had somehow restored himself to his old slimness and impeccable tailoring, although his hair was still thin.

'Get lost,' snarled Agatha.

He put his foot in the door. 'I need a shoulder to cry on,' he said.

Agatha hesitated and then opened the door wide. 'Come in, but make it quick. I was just about to go out.'

He followed her into the kitchen. 'Any chance of a coffee?'

'I'll make some and we'll take our cups into the garden. It's a glorious day. Don't spoil it by staying too long.'

'If you say so,' said Charles gloomily.

Agatha made two mugs of instant coffee and they carried them out into the garden and sat at a table in the sunshine.

'So,' began Agatha, 'what's up?'

'She's left me.'

'What! Your wife? The French bird? Why?'

'Would you believe it, Aggie, she says it's because I'm mean. She's gone to Paris and says she doesn't want to see me again.'

'Well, you always were tight with money, Charles. When it comes to paying a bill in a restaurant, you've always managed to forget your wallet.'

'I'm thrifty,' he said defensively. 'And she's got oodles of cash, but she says she sees no reason why she should have to spend her own.'

'You sound like soul mates,' commented Agatha drily. Her stomach gave a rumble. 'I've got to eat something,' she said.

'Then I'll prove to you I'm a reformed character. I'll take you for dinner. What do you feel like?'

Agatha felt for a moment that she should rebuff him. He had behaved disgracefully. But then, when had Charles ever behaved well?

'Oh, all right. I feel like Chinese. There's a good restaurant in Evesham. I'll go and change.'

'So what have you been up to?' asked Charles as they tackled pancakes and crispy duck.

'It's an odd business,' said Agatha. 'Did you read about that girl found in the river in Evesham?'

'Saw something about it. Tell me. This is like old times.'

Yes, it was, thought Agatha. She almost expected James to walk in the door. He'd had a habit of turning up when she was with Charles.

Agatha started first with meeting Kylie at the beauticians. Charles listened carefully until she had finished.

'What a complicated case!' he exclaimed when she finally fell silent. 'I think you should concentrate more on this Marilyn Josh. She lives at the same address as Harry McCoy.

Someone saw you and decided to kill you, or that someone decided to phone the murderer and say where you were. Kylie was black-mailing Barrington. Who knows? She may have been blackmailing someone else.'

'But who? Someone we don't know?'

'And this Joanna Field. Wouldn't her neigh-bours have seen anything?'

'I don't know that she has any neighbours. She lives above a shop in Port Street. A lot of property there is still flood-damaged, you know, no one doing anything until the insur-ance comes through, and with so many claims, that could take ages. Anyway, the police will already have interviewed everyone possible. I feel something awful has happened to her.'

'Maybe not. Maybe she just wanted to clear off knowing the police would want to question her about Barrington.'

'Without clothes or money?'

'She could have been very frightened.'

'She didn't strike me as being frightened the last time I saw her. Angry, cheeky, insolent. But not frightened.'

'Let's look at the drug business. That sug-gests viciousness plus organization.'

'That brings us back to the club again and there's no record of any drugs being dealt there.'

'Needn't be the club. What about Barring-ton's? Barrington himself sounds a nasty bit of work, and what about that goon you described, George, the one who mans the front desk?'

'Really, Charles. A plumbing business?'

'All things are possible. Would they have a deep freeze at Barrington's?'

'I shouldn't think so. Anyway, after the blackmailing business came out, the police would have turned the place inside out. I wish it would turn out to be Phyllis.'

'Why that one?'

'She's a narcissistic bully. She's violently jealous. She hated Kylie. I think she's a low life.'

'Any sign that she takes drugs?'

'Not that I noticed, but unless someone has bare arms and track marks up them, I wouldn't know.'

'Tell you what. Why don't I stay the night and I'll go round all these people with you tomorrow?'

'No, Charles. I've got to serve teas in the village tomorrow for some photographic exhibition.' Agatha hesitated. It was difficult to continue to be angry with the lightweight Charles. And somehow, just talking over a case with him like old times connected her in some way to James Lacey. 'But I tell you what. Why don't you call over on Saturday and we'll take it from there?'

'Great. I'll come in the morning and we'll get started.'

'What are you going to do about your marriage?'

'What about it?'

'I mean, aren't you going to try to fix things? Fly to Paris?'

'No point. I mean, it's not just her I have to deal with. It's her father, mother, two brothers, uncles, aunts, all jabbering at me in French.'

'But Charles. She's expecting twins!'

A faint red flush crept up Charles's face. Agatha stared at him in amazement. 'You're actually blushing! I didn't think you could.'

'The fact is,' he said, twisting the stem on his wineglass, 'I got well and truly caught.'

'How?'

'I met her when I was on holiday in Saint Tropez. She was well-guarded by relatives, friends and family, and although she was – is – awfully pretty, I wouldn't have made a move if she hadn't moved on me. She kept gazing over at me in this restaurant, sending out signals. You know. One day, she was on her own. I stopped at her table and asked if she was enjoying her stay. She asked me to sit down. We laughed and talked. Then she saw her parents coming into the restaurant and asked me quickly where I was staying. I gave her the name of my hotel. She said she'd meet me in the foyer at midnight. And she did. And we spent the night together, although she had to sneak off at six in the morning. She told me she was on the pill. No, I didn't have any protection. To tell the truth, I didn't know I was going to need it. I didn't see her again and put it all down to a rather intriguing one-night stand. I'd given her my address and phone number. A month later I got this hysterical phone call from Paris saying her period was late and that she'd lied to me about being on the pill. I told her to check out whether she was pregnant or not and phone me back. She phoned back a day later and confirmed that she was. Well, I decided to do the decent thing. Family's rich, she's pretty, chance to be a dad, all that. Went over, met the family, popped the question. Got a bit frightened with marriage settlements and lawyers before the wedding and asked her if she was really sure she was pregnant and she smiled at me mistily and said she had been told she was expecting twins.

'Well, that clinched it. I could see myself teaching them to fish and ride and Daddy stuff like that. Went ahead with the wedding. Only realize now in retrospect that I'd told her a lot about me but she hadn't told me that much about her past. Anyway, by the time we got married, she should have been about four months preggers but she didn't really look pregnant, but she was on this salad diet because she said she didn't want to get too fat. So we got married and I took her back to Warwickshire, where she was bored out of her tiny mind. It was my aunt – remember her? – who began nagging me about her not showing any signs at all of pregnancy. I began to get suspicious and made an appointment for her with a gynaecologist in London and then told her that she should get checked up and see if everything was okay. She began to rant and rave that I was mean, that she hadn't expected to stay buried in the country. That was when I accused her of cheating me, of not being pregnant at all.

'She insisted sulkily that she'd thought she was. I said, so what about these twins? She said the doctor must have made a mistake. She was going back to Paris and wanted a divorce. I said she could get one if she took all the blame. God, I never realized what she was really like. She pointed out, quite rightly, that there was nothing on record that she was pregnant. And there wasn't! She had made me swear not to tell her parents. After the wedding I said, "Let's tell them now," and she said, "Oh, no, Maman and Papa would be so shocked." And to think I went along with it!

'I mean, she certainly was no virgin when I'd first had her. I felt stuck, and I would have been stuck if it hadn't been for my man, Gustav.'

'He's back with you, is he?' Agatha remembered Charles's terrifying butler.

'Yes, and terribly keen on gadgets is old Gustav. I kept forgetting appointments, dinners and things that people had phoned up to invite me to. So Gustav bought this thingy that plugs into your phone and records things.

He went over the tapes and glory be, there were the two calls from her saying she thought she was pregnant and then the one saying she had been to the doctor and it had been confirmed.

'Anyway, my lawyers are dealing with it and I don't want to see her or anyone from France again.'

'Why pick on you?'

'That's where it gets interesting.'

'I thought it was all already interesting enough,' commented Agatha.

'Boofy Pratt-Rogers, an old school friend of mine who works at the British Embassy in Paris, got the low-down. Anne-Marie Duchenne, that's the wife, had one flaming affair with some French comte. Can't remember his name. They were supposed to get married and were engaged and all and then this comte ups and offs at the last minute and marries someone else. Anne-Marie devastated and furious and with a bad case of the "I'll show him." Family take her to Saint Trop to recover and she's tipped off that I'm a rich English milord. Of course I'm only a baronet, but what does a Frog know?' said Charles with a burst of xenophobic bitterness.

'Mrs Bloxby would say,' said Agatha, 'that the good Lord was punishing you for years of philandering.'

'Mrs Bloxby would not say anything so unkind. Shall we go?'

'After you've paid the bill,' said Agatha.

Charles had parked a little way down the High Street from the restaurant. Agatha was walking along to the car with him when she suddenly came face to face with Marilyn Josh. She quickly ducked her head and scurried along to the car. Open the door, Charles, quickly, her mind pleaded as he fumbled for his keys. Just before Agatha slid into the passenger seat, she glanced back. Marilyn was standing looking along the street at her.

'Lost something?' asked Charles as Agatha crouched down.

'No, that was Marilyn Josh on the High Street, just before we reached the car. She was looking straight at me, and when I got into the car I looked back, and she was standing in the High Street staring at me.'

'I thought you were wearing some disguise when you interviewed her.'

'Yes, a blond wig and glasses. It really did alter my appearance.'

'Were you by any chance wearing the clothes you're wearing now?'

Agatha glanced down at her biscuit-coloured trouser-suit. 'Lord, I was wearing this last time I saw her.'

'Can't be helped. She probably thought there was something familiar about you, but couldn't quite think what.'

'Let's hope so,' said Agatha.

* * *

Charles had left and she was preparing for bed when the phone rang. It was Bill Wong. 'The most peculiar thing has happened, Agatha,' he said. 'We've just arrested two young fellows high on drugs, who frightened the life out of a woman in Mircester by driving straight at her. She said she jumped clear and was able to give us a description of the car and the licence number. Tough old bird with nerves of steel. So we picked them up. The car was stolen. They're being charged with that, plus possession of drugs. Now Worcester police are going to have to be brought into this because they'll want to know if they were the ones who killed Mrs Anstruther-Jones. They could be the ones that went for you.'

'Don't tell Brudge about me,' pleaded Agatha.

'I can't very well tell him now,' said Bill, 'and more's the pity. They're trying to say they only did it to give her a fright, just a joke, they would have slammed on the brakes at the last minute. There's been a few more instances of this kind of thing. We'll need to sweat it out of them, find the other cars they've stolen and try to get forensics to come up with something. It could be that the attack on you was just these silly buggers playing games.'

'What about Mrs Anstruther-Jones?'

'Could be them as well and it was a joke that went wrong. I'll let you know.'

Agatha, after she had rung off, found herself

hoping that it had been them. But before she fell asleep, Marilyn Josh's face rose before her eyes. She could only hope she hadn't recognized her.

The following day was sultry and warm. The sun was veiled in thin cloud. The leaves on the trees hung motionless. What a day for standing behind a counter with a hot tea urn and a hot coffee urn, Agatha thought crossly.

She put on a loose summer gown and made her way along to the hall. At the back of the hall, tables and chairs had been laid out to make a temporary tea-room. There was a long trestletable filled with home-made cakes and sandwiches and the urns of tea and coffee.

Three o'clock arrived. Agatha shifted restlessly in the heat. Very few people were coming in. The school hall smelled of dust and chalk. Dust motes drifted in shafts of sunlight.

Mrs Bloxby, who had been selling tickets at the school hall door, surrendered her post to Miss Simms and joined Agatha. 'It's quite sad,' she said. 'Poor Mr Parry. That's him over there.'

Agatha looked to where a stooped, elderly gentleman was standing in front of one of his photographs.

'Who's he?'

'Mr Parry is the man whose collection of old photographs it is. So sad. I would have thought more people would have been interested.'

'Take over from me,' said Agatha. 'I'll have this place full in an hour.'

She went to a cupboard where she knew materials were kept for finger-painting, having once been drafted by Mrs Bloxby to supervise a kindergarten class while the teacher went to the doctor. She pulled out a large square of cardboard and painted FREE TEAS, HOME-BAKING, CHURCH HALL, ALL WELCOME on the card. She went to her car and drove up to the main road and tacked the card on to a tree. Then she went back to the hall.

'We're giving away the teas and stuff,' she told Mrs Bloxby. 'Don't panic. I'll pay you for them.'

'That's awfully generous of you. Are you sure?'

'Real little Lady Bountiful, me,' said Agatha with a shrug. 'Anything to liven this dump up.'

Cars started to arrive and then a whole coach-load of people. Mrs Bloxby was once more at the door, saying sweetly, 'It's two pounds for admission, but that covers your afternoon teas.' Agatha grinned. The vicar's wife had jacked up the price from twenty pee. Then she was kept so busy serving that the rest of the afternoon flew past until every cake and sandwich had gone. Old Mr Parry had spent a happy time taking people round his exhibition of pictures.

'I think you've done enough, Mrs Raisin,' beamed Mrs Bloxby. 'The ladies and I will clean up.'

'Thanks,' said Agatha with relief. 'I'm so hot and sticky, I need a bath.'

'Oh, before you go, Mr Parry would really like to show you his photographs. He says you've been working so hard you haven't had enough time to see them.'

'Must I?'

'I said you would.'

'Rats!'

Agatha slouched off to join Mr Parry. 'Ah, Mrs Raisin,' he cried. 'Shall we start with this one? This is a view of Blockley High Street circa 1910, and this . . .'

Agatha's mind drifted off in the heat. At last the tour was over. 'Thank you very much,' said Agatha.

'I didn't display them all,' he said. 'Some I have in a folder were watermarked or cracked, but very interesting for all that.'

To Agatha's horror he picked up a folder from a chair, opened it and spread the contents on a table. 'I have an appointment,' she gabbled. 'Must go.'

He looked at her in disappointment. 'I'm sure they're all as fascinating as the ones in the exhibition,' she said, 'but . . .'

On the top of the open folder was a sepia

photograph of a street which seemed familiar to her. In the next second, she realized it was the back lane where the disco was situated. But where the disco now stood there was a butcher's shop, with the butcher grinning outside and game hanging from hooks.

'A butcher,' said Agatha.

He gave her a peculiar look. 'Yes, obviously. So few of the old butchers left now that people go to the supermarket. That was Gringe's. Bless me, that's an old photograph, but they were there until five years ago. They sold up. The man that bought it meant to turn it into two flats but he went bankrupt and it was sold to those disco people. Such a shame.'

Agatha walked off slowly, deaf to his cry of 'But you haven't seen the others!'

A butcher, thought Agatha. How far would the chap who bought it for the flats have got with the conversion? Say he hadn't got anywhere, then it would be as it had been when it was a butcher's shop. That would mean the walk-in deep freeze would still be there.

'Mrs Raisin!'

Agatha turned round reluctantly. It was Mrs Bloxby. 'Mr Parry thought you'd taken a funny turn.'

'I'm all right. It was one of those photographs, Mrs Bloxby. A butchers used to be in Evesham where the disco is now and that means there still might be a deep freeze there.'

'But the police searched the disco!'

'They were looking for a freezer chest,' said Agatha excitedly. 'What if the freezer room is still there, behind a curtain or a fake wall?'

'You must tell the police.'

'Gringe was the name of the butcher. I'm going to see if I can find the man who sold the shop and get him to draw me a plan of where that freezer room was. Then I'll go to the disco tomorrow night and see if it's still there.'

'Mrs Raisin, it's too dangerous.'

'You mustn't tell the police. This is my case,' said Agatha fiercely. 'Promise?'

'I promise,' said Mrs Bloxby reluctantly.

As soon as she got home, Agatha checked the phone-book. There were two Gringes, A. Gringe and M. Gringe.

She dialled the A. Gringe. No reply. She tried the M. Gringe. A woman answered. Agatha said she wanted to speak to whoever had owned the butcher's shop which was now a disco. 'Oh, that's my husband's father,' she said.

'Do you know when he'll be at home?' asked Agatha. 'I phoned him but there was no reply.'

'He doesn't go out much. He's probably out in his garden.'

'I see he lives in Badsey,' said Agatha.

'Yes, you'll find his house is near the school-house. Know where that is?'

Agatha said she did and rang off.

She had a quick shower and changed. Before she left for Badsey, she phoned Charles's number to put him off. Agatha wanted all the glory for herself. Gustav answered the phone and said Sir Charles was out and so she left a message. Now for Mr Gringe.

His home in Badsey was a trim, end-of-terrace house. Agatha saw there was a path at the side leading to the garden at the back, and decided to try the garden first.

She walked along the path. The garden was a plantless miracle. A wooden deck stretched out from behind the back door covered in a canvas canopy, and the area in front of it, where an old man was stooped, pulling at a weed, was covered in small shiny pebbles.

'Mr Gringe?'

He straightened up, his eyes roaming over the pebbles as if threatening any other bit of green to show its face. 'Yes?'

'I'm Agatha Raisin. I want to ask you about your butcher's shop, the one that's now a disco.'

He turned slowly and looked at her. His face was seamed and lined and his shoulders were stooped. He wiped his hands on an old pair of flannels, held one out and solemnly shook Agatha's hand.

'What do you want to know?'

'I wondered if you could draw me a plan of

your shop as it once was, showing me where the freezer, the cold room, was situated.'

'Why?'

'I'm writing a book,' lied Agatha, 'and I have this butcher's shop in it. I need a layout.'

'So why don't you just go to the butchers in, say, Moreton, and ask them to show you around?'

'Because I'm setting it in the past,' said Agatha desperately. 'I need an old-fashioned butcher's shop.'

He indicated a gleaming white plastic table surrounded by hard plastic chairs on the deck. 'Let's sit down and I'll get a piece of paper.'

Agatha sat down and he shuffled off into the house. He seemed to be gone a very long time. She waited impatiently.

At last he reappeared, holding a sheet of white A4 paper and a ball-point pen. He sat down beside her with painstaking slowness and then said, 'Let me see, the counter was here as you came in the door. Had to be a cold counter, you know, glassed in. Bloody European regulations!' He began to draw with neat, draughtsmanlike precision.

'Through this door behind the counter was a short corridor and then a big area at the back. Deliveries came in by the back door. We cut up the meat in this room. There was a toilet here, and then a kitchen.'

'The freezer?' prompted Agatha.

'The cold room was just here, at the end of

the large room at the back. Inconvenient place, but it would have cost too much to move it.' His pen moved on, neatly sketching everything in. Agatha waited patiently while he drew a plan of the upstairs as well.

'Those disco people got it cheap,' he grumbled, 'because of all the conversion they'd have to do. I wanted to sell it to a butcher, but what butchers are there nowadays? The supermarkets have killed most of us off. The last straw was the E. coli scare. And the beef-on-the-bone scare. Couldn't sell a joint of meat on the bone anywhere, and that took extra butchering time. Damn government. You put that in your book. The government helped to kill us off, us and the farmers. I'd shoot the lot of them. Want a drink?'

Agatha decided, as she had not planned to go to the disco until the next evening, the least she could do would be to give him some more of her time. 'That would be nice.' She was just about to say she would have a gin and tonic, when he added, 'I make the best dandelion wine in the Cotswolds.' Agatha resigned herself.

He shuffled indoors again. Birds chirped sleepily in the neighbouring gardens but no bird sang in Mr Gringe's stark garden. The evening sky stretched overhead, a pale green deepening to dark blue at the horizon. Somewhere deep inside her, a voice was telling her she was being dangerously silly, that she

236

should turn over everything she had to the police.

Mr Gringe came shuffling back carrying a tray with a bottle and two glasses. He poured out two large glasses of dandelion wine. 'Here's to you,' he said. Agatha raised her glass. 'Good health.'

'So what name do you write under?' he asked.

'Agatha Raisin.'

'Never heard of you.'

'Do you read much?'

'No, I've got the telly.'

'Then that's why you haven't heard of me.' Agatha looked out over the garden. 'Don't you like plants?'

'Waste of time. They get aphids and slugs and then they're always dropping leaves and making a mess.'

'Some people think it worth the effort to look out at pretty flowers.'

'Some people need their heads examined. Are you married?'

'Divorced.'

'Have you any money?'

'I'm comfortably off.'

He suddenly leered at her. 'Don't do to be on your own. Tell you what. You can marry me. I'm tired of all the cleaning and scrubbing, and that's women's work.'

'Then you should employ a cleaner.'

'Pay someone to do it? No, that's where you come in.'

'And this is where I go out,' said Agatha firmly, putting her glass on the table. The wine was sweet and heavy and she did not think she could bear to swallow another sip.

'You're missing out,' he called after her as she snatched up the plan of the butcher's shop and made for the side of the house and escape. 'You're lucky to get an offer at your age.'

Chapter Ten

Mrs Bloxby called on Agatha the following evening, just as Agatha was ready to go out. The vicar's wife gloomily surveyed Agatha in full disguise. 'You're actually going to do it?'

'Of course,' said Agatha calmly, just as if she had not been wrestling with doubts and fears all day.

'Is it any use me trying to point out to you that you are putting your life in danger?'

'None whatsoever. Anyway, I'm only going to locate the place – if they still have the freezer room. Then I'll leave and phone the police.'

They walked outside together. 'I'll be all right,' said Agatha, getting into her car. 'I tell you what. If I'm not back by midnight, then you can phone the police.'

Agatha parked in the car-park at Merstow Green and studied Mr Gringe's map. It was going to be difficult. Terry Jensen had obviously had the wall that had existed between the front and back premises knocked down to make room for the disco. Did the disco dance-room extend right through to the back door? Or was there still a space left at the back with a hidden door somewhere? There might be. Goods might be delivered at the back door.

Agatha got out of the car, wishing now she had let Charles come with her. She felt very alone.

Wayne, the bouncer, was standing outside the club. 'Television again,' said Agatha briskly. 'Just going to soak up the atmosphere.'

Wayne stood aside to let her pass. The disco was quieter than the last time Agatha had been there. There were fewer couples gyrating on the floor, although the music was still as loud as ever. She hoped it would soon fill up to disguise the fact that she would be searching around the walls. She went to the bar where Terry was on duty. She shouted at him that she was just getting a feel of the place and ordered a bottle of beer. As she sipped her beer, she looked carefully round about. Then she thought, there must be a toilet somewhere. It might be situated in the back premises. 'Got a ladies' room?' she shouted at Terry.

He opened a door at the side of the bar which Agatha had not noticed before because it was part of a painted mural of a dancing couple. He jerked his head. Agatha walked through. 'On the left,' he shouted.

There were two toilets, one marked 'Gals' and the other, 'Guys'. As he was still watching her, Agatha went into the 'Gals' and into one of the cubicles. She sat down on the lavatory seat and took her map out and studied it again. Outside had been dark except for dim lights above the toilet doors. Surely Terry would have gone by now. He couldn't watch every woman who decided to go to the toilet.

Agatha made her way out and looked quickly around. Beer crates and cases of soft drinks were stacked against the opposite wall. She looked at her map again. If the freezer room was still there, it would be behind those crates and cases. Quickly, she began to move them away from the wall, panting with the effort. The wall behind was covered with a dirty curtain. She paused in her efforts and tried the back door. It wasn't locked. Good, thought Agatha. If I find something, I can escape that way. It was when she started on the cases in the central section that she realized they were empty. She began to throw them behind her, confident that the music from the disco would cover the noise. What if someone came in to use one of the toilets? But she would have to risk it. She would think of some excuse. She would scream and say she had seen a rat. When she had cleared a big enough space, she lifted the curtain and peered underneath. It was too dark to see anything. She fumbled in her handbag until she located a pencil torch. She shone it up and down the wall.

And then her heart began to thump. There was a wooden door with a metal handle. The freezer room. She ducked under the curtain and seized the handle and pulled the heavy door open, to be met by a blast of icy air. Agatha went inside. She fumbled inside the door for a light switch until she found it and pressed it down. Fluorescent strip lighting snapped on overhead.

Agatha let out a cry of pure terror.

Sitting on the floor with her head at an awkward angle was Joanna Field. Agatha put a hand up to her lips. Move! screamed her brain. Get out! Get the police. The air was full of the thud of the disco music pounding in her ears. And then there was a louder thud. She swung round. The door had been slammed shut behind her.

'Something's worrying me, Alf,' said Mrs Bloxby.

'What is it, dear?' asked the vicar.

'It's about Agatha Raisin.'

'Oh, that silly woman. What's she been up to now?'

Mrs Bloxby explained about Agatha's visit to the disco and why she had gone.

'Then you must tell the police immediately,' said the vicar.

'She made me promise I wouldn't.'

The doorbell rang. 'Maybe that's her,' said

Mrs Bloxby. She hurried to open the door. John Armitage stood there. 'I've just got back from London,' he said. 'Where's Agatha?'

'Come in,' urged Mrs Bloxby. 'I'd better tell you.'

She repeated what she had just told her husband. 'You said you wouldn't tell the police,' said John when she had finished. 'I didn't.'

'The phone's over there,' said Mrs Bloxby eagerly.

John phoned Worcester police, was put through to Brudge and began to talk rapidly, ending up with 'You must get men there now. Her life could be in danger.'

He finally put down the phone. 'They'll get there as quickly as possible. I'm going there myself.'

'We'll go with you,' said Mrs Bloxby, ignoring the vicar's pleas that any rescue should be left to the police. They piled into the vicar's ancient Morris Minor and headed for Evesham.

'Can't this car of yours go any faster?' asked John at one point.

'I am not ruining my engine for one silly woman,' remarked the vicar.

Agatha walked up and down, desperately beating her arms at her sides. What a way to end! Frozen to death. And poor Joanna. She must have found something incriminating in

Kylie's e-mails and tried to blackmail them. Agatha felt sick with cold and despair. She was about to die and all because of vanity. She had wanted to solve the case herself, have all the glory. She would never see James again. There were shelves inside the room stacked with boxes. She pulled open one with frozen fingers and found plastic packets of white powder. So this was where they kept the drugs. Kylie must have known. Kylie must have found out. Poor Kylie. Poor Joanna. And poor Agatha.

The shivering finally stopped and she began to feel sleepy and almost warm. She had a paradoxical desire to take all her clothes off and fought against it.

The vicar parked up on the pavement outside the disco and the three got out. Wayne blocked their way as they tried to walk into the disco. 'It's for young people only,' he said truculently.

'Then I shall report you immediately to the police for ageism,' said the vicar loftily.

Wayne gave him a hunted look but the word 'police' acted as an open sesame. They walked into the disco. Music assailed their ears. Couples were dancing. It all looked very normal, except that they could not see Agatha. John shouldered his way towards the bar, with the Bloxbys close behind. 'Where's the television researcher?' he demanded. Terry gave a final polish to a glass. 'You've just missed her,' he shouted. 'Left ten minutes ago.'

John gave him a baffled look. Agatha could be up in the office.

He swung round and shouted to Alf, 'What can we do now?'

'I have prayed,' said the vicar calmly. 'The police will be here.'

'Praying's a fat lot of good,' shouted John but the words were no sooner out of his mouth than the music suddenly died and the disco was full of police, headed by Brudge.

Terry had turned a muddy colour. John thought quickly. If there was a cold room left over from the days when there had been a butcher's shop, it would be on ground level.

'Through the back,' he said to Brudge. 'There must be some way through the back.'

'There's a door here, sir,' said a policeman with sharper eyes than Agatha Raisin.

'That's the toilets, and the stores, nothing else,' said Terry.

'Watch him and see he doesn't get away,' said Brudge. He walked through the door beside the bar. He took out a torch and shone it around, shone it up and down the stack of soft-drink cases and beer crates and then on the floor. He saw faint scrape marks on the floor, as if someone had pulled the cases back. Then he remembered in a report when the disco had been searched that said behind the crates there was an old freezer room, but it had been full of stores and junk and the refrigerator unit had been disconnected.

'Move those crates and cases as fast as you can,' he barked at his men. 'And pull down that curtain behind them.'

Inside, shivering Agatha had realized that there was no longer the dim thud of the music. She heard the crates being moved from behind the door. She heard voices. She did not scream because she was sure they had come to make sure she wasn't going to live any longer. From the looks of Joanna, someone had broken her neck.

Agatha looked around for a weapon. But there was nothing.

She would never forget the moment when the door swung open and she found herself staring at Detective Inspector Brudge. 'Oh, you lovely man,' cried Agatha and flung herself sobbing into his arms.

Brudge pried himself loose. 'Get her to an ambulance,' he barked, 'and search this place. My God, that's the missing girl!'

Agatha then was embraced by Mrs Bloxby, who wrapped her in the vicar's jacket. 'I'm a fool,' sobbed Agatha.

'There, now,' soothed Mrs Bloxby. 'It's all over.'

An ambulance arrived and Agatha was wrapped up and stretchered in. A policewoman got in beside her.

Mrs Bloxby caught hold of the ambulance

driver as he was about to climb into the ambulance. 'Will she be all right?' she asked.

'I think so,' he said. 'She seems to be suffering from moderate hypothermia.'

The ambulance roared off.

Agatha recovered quickly and awoke from a refreshing sleep two days later just as Brudge and two detectives entered the hospital room. 'Strong enough to make a statement?' asked Brudge.

The one thing Agatha lied about was her reasons for not phoning the police. She said it was such a long shot that she decided to have a look herself.

At last, when the statement was over, Agatha said, 'But why?'

'Why what?'

'I guess they killed Kylie because she'd found out about the drugs. But why not leave her body where it was and then take it out some dark night and bury it?'

Brudge signalled to the others to leave and settled back in a chair beside the bed. 'May as well tell you the whole thing. Zak cracked. What happened was this. He really did mean to marry Kylie and he was in love with her. But idiot that he was, he told her about the drugs. Now he and his father had no previous criminal records. But one of the major Birmingham gangs heard about him setting up the disco in

Evesham. They approached Terry Jensen with an offer. If he stored the drugs for them, he'd be a very rich man. He wasn't to distribute them in the disco. He was merely to store them so they could be picked up and distributed elsewhere in the Midlands. Now Zak may have been in love with Kylie, but Kylie doesn't seem to have been in love with Zak. She thought this little bit of information was gold and began to demand all sorts of things from Terry, like, after they were married, she wanted a Ferrari.

'Terry told Zak she'd have to go. He was appalled, but it was either Kylie, or himself and his father serving a long prison sentence. She had been bitching about the wedding gown and somehow he persuaded her to slip out one night and bring it round to the club. They'd switched off the refrigeration in the cold room. Told her to go in there – they had it uncovered – and try it on. Then they shut the door and locked it and turned on the refrigeration. With all she had drunk, it made the process of hypothermia quicker.'

'But wouldn't her hands have been bruised, hammering on the door?' asked Agatha.

'There were no injuries to her arms. I think she thought they were playing a joke on her until it was too late. When she was weak enough, they injected her with heroin.'

'But why the river and why the bouquet?'

'Zak was sick with misery. He had loved her. He wanted her to have a more ceremonious burial than the one his father had planned for her. He bought the roses – where, we still don't know. Somehow he got her to the river, still in her wedding gown, and as a last farewell, he thrust the bouquet into her frozen hands. I think he must have been a bit off his head with grief, because he thought, in all the chaos of the floods, that it might be assumed she was another flood victim, wedding dress and all.'

'And what about Joanna?' asked Agatha.

'They got tipped off – we're still trying to find out who did that – and someone struck her as she was getting into Kylie's e-mail and then wiped all the e-mails out. But Joanna did find one incriminating e-mail before she was hit. Zak says he sent her a desperate e-mail, saying to keep her mouth shut.

'Joanna knew she was on to something. She called round at the disco and told Terry about the e-mail and that unless he paid up, she was going to go to the police. He broke her neck.'

'And Mrs Anstruther-Jones?'

'It could be youths who made a habit of getting high on drugs and frightening people by driving at them. They may have gone too far. Zak denies they had anything to do with it, but Terry, or that Wayne, may have thought it was you and decided to stop you asking questions about Kylie.'

'There's one thing I totally forgot,' said Agatha. 'Kylie was a member of a church group. I should have asked about her there.'

'We are not completely inept,' retorted Brudge. 'We did, of course, question the members. Kylie went once and then never again, although her mother believed her to be a staunch member.'

Agatha lay back against the pillows, her brow wrinkled. 'There's something missing,' she said slowly. 'Or rather, someone.'

'What do you mean?'

Agatha lay back in silence for a moment. Then she said, 'I asked Freda Stokes if Kylie had been particularly friendly with any of the girls and she said no. I asked her about wedding presents. She said that Marilyn Josh had given Kylie a thong swim-suit. Now it must have seemed like a shocking present to Freda, who at that time considered her daughter a respectable virgin. But what if it was something that Kylie really wanted? When I first saw her, she was getting a bikini wax. She said it was because Zak wanted it, but maybe Kylie wanted it to sport her swim-suit on her honeymoon. You see,' went on Agatha eagerly, 'Marilyn might have been in on it. She might have known Kylie very well. I think Zak or Terry got her, at the hen party, to whisper to her to bring the wedding dress round to the disco and she'd let her know what she thought.'

'Zak said nothing about Marilyn Josh,' said Brudge, 'but we'll check it out. Here's Mrs Bloxby.'

Brudge stood up to leave.

'Aren't you going to thank me?' asked Agatha.

'For what? For nearly getting killed? For interfering in police business? You're damn lucky you're not being charged. You were wearing that wig again when we found you.'

'Oh, sod off!' shouted Agatha to his retreating back.

'That wasn't very nice, Mrs Raisin,' said Mrs Bloxby reprovingly.

'He deserved it,' said Agatha sulkily.

'You seem to be back on your old form.' The vicar's wife sat down beside the bed. 'It's in all the newspapers and on television.'

'What do they say about me?'

'Nothing, I'm afraid. Just about Kylie and Joanna and that a large quantity of drugs was found at the disco.'

'That does take the biscuit! They'd never have found out if it hadn't been for me,' complained Agatha. 'Where's John?'

'Coming along later.'

'Really! Can you get me my handbag out of that locker? I've got make-up in it.'

'When are they going to release you?' said Mrs Bloxby, retrieving Agatha's capacious handbag and handing it to her.

'Tomorrow,' said Agatha, taking out a small mirror and squinting at her face in it. 'I look a fright.'

She busily began to apply foundation cream. 'Do you think that's a spot coming on my forehead?'

'Can't see anything,' said Mrs Bloxby. 'I've brought you a box of chocolates.'

'How kind of you.' Agatha eyed the box greedily. She loved chocolates but hated the effect even one had on her imagination. One chocolate and she could feel her stomach expanding and her hips grower wider. Still, she had gone through a lot and she deserved at least a few.

She applied powder and lipstick and then opened the box. 'Have one.'

'I've just had breakfast.'

'Oh, go on,' urged Agatha. 'I'll feel like a pig eating them myself.'

Mrs Bloxby took one and Agatha took one and ate it and then reached for another.

They chatted about village affairs, and when Mrs Bloxby at last stood up to leave, Agatha realized that the chocolate box was nearly empty and Mrs Bloxby had only eaten two.

John Armitage arrived in the afternoon, bearing a large bouquet of flowers which Agatha studied carefully until she had judged they were slightly more expensive than the ones he had taken to Joanna.

'Have you heard the latest?' he asked.

'No, what's that?'

'I heard it on the radio. They've rounded up the gang in Birmingham, the ones that got Terry Jensen to store the stuff.'

'And Brudge never even said thank you,' said Agatha.

'I think he got the impression that you were interfering. But you'll have your moment at the trial.'

'Me! If I hadn't interfered, as you put it, he'd still be none the wiser.'

'It's certainly been quite a case. How are you feeling?'

'Fine. I'm out of here tomorrow.'

'I'll take you for dinner to celebrate.'

Agatha brightened. 'That'll be nice. Where?'

'There's a French restaurant in Oxford, Ma Belle, in Blue Boar Street. They've got tables set out in a courtyard in front of the restaurant, and if the weather stays fine, we can go there. I'll pick you up at seven.'

After he had left, Bill Wong arrived with more flowers. 'Agatha,' he said, 'I hope this is the last time I have to visit you in hospital after a case. You did a very dangerous thing.'

'Does that man Brudge do nothing but complain about me?' demanded Agatha furiously.

'I called at the vicarage yesterday. It's Mrs Bloxby who's worried about you. If John Armitage hadn't decided to call the police, you would have been frozen meat.'

But Agatha, as usual, was not going to take the blame for anything. She gave him a long speech about the fact that it was due to her own brilliance that the police had wound up such a successful case.

'That's an expensive bouquet,' said Bill, who had not really been listening to her and was pointing to John's offering.

'It's from John Armitage,' said Agatha proudly. 'He's taking me out for dinner tomorrow night.'

'Be careful.'

'I'm not a virgin.'

'It's just you had enough pain and trouble over falling in love with your last neighbour.'

'I'm not going to fall in love with John Armitage,' howled Agatha.

But the next day, as she left the hospital to be driven home by Mrs Bloxby in the old Morris Minor, Agatha made polite conversation while all the time her mind was plotting and planning what to wear for dinner that evening.

Once home, she resisted the impulse to rush out and buy something new. She had plenty of clothes. It was just a matter of choosing the right things. After having taken every item out of her wardrobe, she settled for a deep-crimson silk evening skirt, slit up the side, and a soft white silk blouse with a plunging neckline.

That evening, made up with care, scented, hair brushed and burnished, she felt she had never looked better. John arrived at seven and they set off for Oxford. It was a warm, glorious evening, with the sun sending down shafts of golden light between the trees, which were still fresh and green, having not yet taken on the dull heaviness of summer.

For once Oxford looked to Agatha like the city of dreaming spires instead of what she usually saw as a mess of a bad traffic system, panhandlers and drunken fourteen-year-olds.

John had booked a table in the courtyard of the restaurant. They ordered their meal and a bottle of wine. They talked about the case, going over and over it, until John asked, 'You seemed to think my book, the one you read, was not quite real. Why was that?'

They were on to their second bottle of wine. Agatha, mellow and secure in his company, began to tell him about her upbringing in the Birmingham slums while he listened, fascinated.

Agatha hardly ever told anyone about this background from which she was so anxious to distance herself.

When she had finished, John ordered brandies and then leaned across the table and gazed into her eyes.

'What about it, Agatha?'

Agatha looked at him, puzzled.

'What about what?'

'You and me making a night of it.'

Agatha still did not understand. 'You mean you want to go on somewhere?'

'Come on, Agatha. You know what I mean. The somewhere is your bed.'

'You've got a cheek,' said Agatha.

'We're both adults.'

Agatha's self-worth, never very high, sank like a stone. It was because she had told him about her upbringing that he thought that no preliminaries were necessary. She rose to her feet. 'Excuse me.'

She walked into the restaurant and past the bar and the diners to a door at the side. She went out into a lane leading up to the High. She hailed a taxi and got in. 'Carsely,' she said. 'Near Moreton-in-Marsh.'

'Cost you,' said the driver.

'Just go!' ordered Agatha.

She was too upset and humiliated even to cry. Not once had John tried to kiss her or show any sign of affection. He had wanted to get laid and she seemed easy.

When she got home, she sat down and switched on her computer and sent an e-mail to Marie, saying that she had changed her mind. She would like to go back to Robinson Crusoe Island. What dates?

Later that evening, she heard her doorbell. She was sure it was John. She put her head under the duvet. The ringing went on for some time. Then, after that, the phone began to ring.

She got out of bed and pulled the jack out of the wall.

She would wait for Marie's reply and then book her planes. Tomorrow, she would pack up her computer and luggage and move to a hotel in London until it was time to leave. She would tell Worcester police where she was and make them promise to tell no one else.

Agatha felt a pang. She would need to leave her cats again, but her cleaner, Doris Simpson, would look after them and they adored Doris.

She felt she hurt all over.

Epilogue

Once more on Robinson Crusoe Island, Agatha sat with Marie and Carlos in the lounge and watched the rain clouds sweep across the bay. It was cold. She should have realized it would be winter in August on the Juan Fernández Islands.

But somehow there was still that atmosphere of peace and comfort, that feeling of being very far away from worries and troubles. Marie and Carlos were good listeners and took Agatha through her story over and over again, until it all seemed so incredible, almost as if it had all never happened.

'This Evesham sounds like a wicked place,' said Marie.

'On the contrary, the people are wonderful. That's what makes it seem so odd,' said Agatha.

'And has this Marilyn Josh been arrested?'

'Yes, I read about it in the newspapers before I left. The police are keeping very quiet about me. I think they don't want anyone to know I was masquerading as a woman from a television company. So I don't get any glory.'

'You get the glory of knowing that a lot of villains are locked up,' pointed out Carlos.

'True,' agreed Agatha, although she privately thought it would have been nice to get some praise and recognition for her efforts.

When Carlos took himself off to go for a long walk, Marie asked, 'And what about your ex-husband?'

'Oh, that's definitely over,' said Agatha. 'I've closed that chapter in my life.'

'So what about this writer who was supposed to be helping you?'

'He insulted me. I don't want to have anything to do with him again.'

'Why?'

'He took me out for dinner. He is very attractive-looking. We went to a restaurant in Oxford.' Agatha broke off and bit her lip.

'So what happened?'

'You may as well know. He wrote a detective story I'd read based in the Birmingham slums, only you don't call them slums any more. You refer to them politely as inner cities. I had said the background didn't ring true and he asked me how I knew.'

'And how did you know?'

May as well tell the truth, thought Agatha. I'm so very far from home.

'Because I was brought up in that sort of environment until I escaped and clawed my way to the top, got a posh accent, got money and success. But my background is something I like to keep quiet about.'

'I do not see why,' said Marie. 'It is a sign of how far you have come by your own efforts.'

'Britain isn't so very class-conscious now, but it was when I was growing up. I've always had this feeling of not fitting in anywhere and that in itself breeds a sort of snobbery. Anyway, I told him because we'd had a fair bit to drink. He propositioned me, just like that. He hadn't uttered one word of praise about my appearance, he hadn't shown me any affection, he hadn't even shown he desired me. So I thought it was because of my poor background that he felt he could dispense with the preliminaries.'

Marie sat like a small round Buddha, lost in thought, her mind going over Agatha's previous stories about the case.

'I remember,' she said, 'that your young friend, this Roy Silver, gave the impression that he was having an affair with you. Yes?'

'Yes, he did.'

'So you are a mature worldly woman who he believes has affairs. A lot of men do not court or woo these days, Agatha. It started in the seventies. Women's magazines urging us to believe that we were the same as men and could behave like men. You can have it all. Do you remember that one? And endless articles about erogenous zones and sexual tricks of the brothel. Women were suddenly even more available for sex than they had ever been before, and so the courtesies between the sexes disappeared. When was the last time you saw a man on public transport stand up to give a woman a seat? And the women were equally to blame. Some even insulted men who held doors open for them. And the dignity of the housewife and mother was taken away. Women who did not work were held in contempt. Children are often brought up by cheap, uncaring help while the mother works.' She sighed. 'Sometimes I feel we women have thrown off one set of chains only to be weighed down by another. I do not think he propositioned you because of your background, but because he, too, had been drinking. He is probably quite naïve where women are concerned. And you must still have been suffering from shock.'

'Perhaps,' said Agatha moodily.

'Were you in love with him?'

'No, he's too cold, too robotic.'

'And could it not be that you misjudged him? You said he'd had an unhappy marriage.'

'No need for him to take it out on me,' said Agatha waspishly. 'He's probably forgotten about the whole thing.'

'Any news of Agatha?' John Armitage asked Mrs Bloxby.

'No, she took off and left her cats at home

for her cleaner to take care of. I think she told Doris Simpson where she was going, but Doris is very loyal and I think Agatha told her not to tell anyone. The near-death experience she had must have overset her. Or,' went on the vicar's wife, 'someone humiliated her. In the past, when Agatha has been hurt, she's always run away.'

She gazed at John with her mild, clear eyes. He fidgeted and turned slightly red.

Mrs Bloxby gave a little sigh. 'You did something, didn't you?'

He gave a reluctant laugh. 'I took her out for dinner in Oxford. We drank a fair bit. I suggested we spend the night together.'

'Just like that?'

'She's not a young girl,' said John defensively, 'and she'd been having an affair with that horrible-looking young man . . .'

'Agatha is not having and never has had an affair with Roy Silver. She is very thin-skinned and doesn't think much of herself. She has also surprisingly old-fashioned ideas when it comes to relationships. Agatha craves affection and romance and you offered a one-night stand. I assume there were no kisses or hand-holding?'

'Women don't need that nowadays.'

'Women will always need that sort of thing.'

'I'll make it up to her when she gets back.'

'Mr Armitage, why don't you just leave her alone?'

He stared at her in surprise.

'I must make some sort of amends.'

'Well, a simple apology should do. But don't chase after her if you're not in love with her.'

'Love?'

'It does exist,' said Mrs Bloxby wearily.

In his office in Worcester, Detective Inspector Brudge had an uneasy conscience. He should have barred that Raisin woman from doing any investigation right from the beginning. He was proud to be a member of the Worcester Police Force, which he considered the best in the country. Now he was having to cover up that small lapse. Of course it had come out about Agatha's masquerade and he had been truthful enough in explaining to his superiors that he had warned her off, but he failed to explain that he had not warned her off in the beginning. Why couldn't the woman go legal? Set up her own detective agency? Get licensed? He might just suggest it.

By the time Agatha boarded the small propeller plane to take her to Santiago, where she planned to spend one night before catching the flight to London, she felt talked out and soothed.

She was finally free of men, free of obsessions. From now on, she would be her own woman. For a start, she would wear sensible shoes and comfortable loose clothes, instead of teetering about on high heels and worrying about her waistline. Her face was shiny and free from make-up.

The captain climbed in behind the controls. He was extremely good-looking. Agatha automatically fumbled in her handbag for her make-up and then decided against it. Give your skin a chance to breathe, she lectured herself crossly.

In Santiago, she checked into the over-furnished Spanish decor of the Hotel Fundador. Not wanting to eat a formal meal by herself in the hotel restaurant, she unpacked the few things she needed for the night and the morning, and made her way to a café-restaurant on O'Higgins Avenue. She opened her Spanish-English dictionary and began to try to translate the food on offer, displayed on coloured placards on the wall. She ordered roast lamb and an avocado salad and a beer.

Distressingly small and beautiful children occasionally tried to make sorties into the café to beg before being chased away. Music was thudding out. Outside on the avenue, crowds sauntered up and down. It was a cold, clear evening.

Agatha's food arrived. To her delight, not only was it cheap, it was delicious.

She felt happy and relaxed, her brain free from worries, anxieties and obsessions.

Agatha raised her glass of beer to her lips.

And then outside, amongst the crowds, James Lacey walked past.

Agatha dropped her glass with a crash. She would have recognized that rangy walk anywhere. Seizing her handbag and deaf to the shout of the waiter, who saw what looked like a customer escaping without paying, she darted out of the door and set off in pursuit.

She thrust her way through the crowds, sometimes losing him, and then seeing that dark head a distance in front of her. The crowd thinned and she put on a desperate spurt.

She caught up with him and seized his arm. 'James!' she panted.

A total stranger turned round and looked down at her, a puzzled look on his face.

Agatha backed off, her face flaming. 'I'm s-sorry,' she stammered. 'M-mistake.'

She turned away from him and scurried back off towards the café, where the waiter who was standing at the door was relieved to see her return.

She asked for her bill. He indicated her half-eaten food on the table. She shook her head, tipped him and paid her bill at the cash desk.

Then she walked slowly back to the hotel.

She went up to her room and fell face-down on the bed.

'Oh, James,' said Agatha. 'Where are you?'

* * *

In the morning, she sat down at a desk in the room and, taking a sheet of hotel stationery, she wrote to James at the Benedictine monastery. She should have thought of it before, she told herself. Of course he was there. It was Marie's questioning that had put the uneasy thought in her head that he might have lied about taking holy orders and becoming a monk.

She kept her letter short and cheerful, ending by asking him if he could send her a note to her home address and let her know how he was getting on. Then she packed her cases and left them for collection and went down to reception and asked them to post the letter for her.

Feeling better now that she had taken some action to find out how he was, Agatha Raisin set out on the long journey home.

If you enjoyed *The Day the Floods Came*, read
on for the first chapter of the next book in the
Agatha Raisin series . . .

Agatha Raisin
AND THE
CURIOUS CURATE

Chapter One

Agatha Raisin was beginning to feel that nothing would ever interest her again. She had
written to a monastery in France, to her ex-
husband, James Lacey, who, she believed, was
taking holy orders, only to receive a letter a
month later saying that they had not heard
from Mr Lacey. Yes, he had left and promised
to return, but they had heard or seen nothing
of him.

So, she thought miserably, James had simply
been sick of her and had wanted a divorce
and had used the monastery as a way to get
out of the marriage. She swore she would
never be interested in a man again, and that
included her neighbour, John Armitage. He
had propositioned her and had been turned
down. Agatha had been hurt because he had
professed no admiration or love for her. They
talked from time to time when they met in
the village, but Agatha refused all invitations
to dinner and so he had finally given up asking her.

So the news that the vicar, Alf Bloxby, was to get a curate buzzed around the village, but left Agatha unmoved. She went regularly to church because of her friendship with the vicar's wife, regarding it more as a duty than anything to do with spiritual uplift. Also because of her friendship with Mrs Bloxby, she felt compelled to attend the Carsely Ladies' Society where the village women discussed their latest fund-raising projects.

It was a warm August evening when Agatha trotted wearily along to the vicarage. She looked a changed Agatha. No make-up, sensible flat sandals and a loose cotton dress.

Miss Simms, the secretary, read the minutes of the last meeting. They were all out in the vicarage garden. Agatha barely listened, watching instead how Miss Simms's stiletto heels sank lower and lower into the grass.

Mrs Bloxby had recently been elected chairwoman. Definitely the title of chairwoman. No chairpersons in Carsely. After tea and cakes had been passed round, she addressed the group. 'As you know, ladies, our new curate will be arriving next week. His name is Tristan Delon and I am sure we all want to give him a warm welcome. We shall have a reception here on the following Wednesday. Everyone in the village of Carsely has been invited.'

'Won't that be rather a crush?' asked Miss Jellop, a thin, middle-aged lady with a lisping voice and large protruding eyes. Agatha thought unkindly that she looked like a rabbit with myxomatosis.

'I don't think there will be all that much interest,' said Mrs Bloxby ruefully. 'I am afraid church attendances are not very high these days.'

Agatha thought cynically that the lure of free food and drinks would bring them in hordes. She wondered whether to say anything, and then a great weariness assailed her. It didn't matter. She herself would not be going. She had recently returned from London, where she had taken on a freelance public relations job for the launch of a new soap called Mystic Health, supposed to be made from Chinese herbs. Agatha had balked at the name, saying that people didn't want healthy soap, they wanted pampering soap, but the makers were adamant. She was about to go back to London for the launch party and intended to stay for a week and do some shopping.

At the end of the following week, Agatha made her way to Paddington station, wondering, as she had wondered before, why London did not hold any magic for her any more. It seemed dusty and dingy, noisy and threatening. She had not particularly enjoyed the launch of the new soap, feeling she was moving in a world to which she no longer belonged. But what was waiting for her in her home village of Carsely? Nothing. Nothing but domestic chores, the ladies' society, and pottering about the village.

But when she collected her car at Moreton-in-Marsh station and began the short drive home, she felt a lightening of her spirits. She would call on Mrs Bloxby and sit in the cool green of the vicarage garden and feel soothed.

Mrs Bloxby was pleased to see her. 'Come in, Mrs Raisin,' she said. Although she and Agatha had been friends for some time, they still used the formal 'Mrs' when addressing each other, a tradition of the ladies' society, which fought a rearguard action against modern times and modern manners. 'Isn't it hot?' exclaimed the vicar's wife, pushing a damp tendril of grey hair away from her face. 'We'll sit in the garden. What is your news?'

Over the teacups Agatha regaled her with a highly embroidered account of her experiences in London. 'And how's the new curate?' she finally asked.

'Getting along splendidly. Poor Alf is laid low with a summer cold and Mr Delon has been taking the services.' She giggled. 'I haven't told Alf, but last Sunday there was standing room only in the church. Women had come from far and wide.'

'Why? Is he such a good preacher?'

'It's not that. More tea? Help yourself to milk and sugar. No, I think it is because he is so very beautiful.'

'Beautiful? A beautiful curate? Is he gay?'

'Now why should you assume that a beautiful young man must be gay?'

'Because they usually are,' said Agatha gloomily.

'No, I don't think he's gay. He is very charming. You should come to church this Sunday and see for yourself.'

'I might do that. Nothing else to do here.'

'I hate it when you get bored,' said the vicar's wife anxiously. 'It seems to me that every time you get bored, a murder happens somewhere.'

'Murder happens every day all over the place.'

'I meant close by.'

'I'm not interested in murders. That last case I nearly got myself killed. I had a letter from that Detective Inspector Brudge in Worcester just before I left. He suggested I should go legit and set up my own detective agency.'

'Now that's a good idea.'

'I would spend my days investigating nasty divorces or working undercover in firms to find out which typist has been nicking the office stationery. No, it's not for me. Is this curate living with you?'

'We found him a room in the village with old Mrs Feathers. As you know, she lives opposite the church, so we were lucky. Of course, we were prepared to house him here, we have plenty of room, but he would not hear of it. He says he is quite comfortably off. He has a small income from a family trust.'

'I'd better get back to my cats,' said Agatha, rising. 'I think they prefer Doris Simpson to me.' Mrs Simpson was Agatha's cleaner, who looked after the cats when Agatha was away.

'So you will come to church on Sunday?' asked Mrs Bloxby. 'I am curious to learn what you make of our curate.'

'Why, I wonder,' said Agatha, her bearlike eyes sharpening with interest. 'You have reservations about him?'

'I feel he's too good to be true. I shouldn't carp. We are very lucky to have him. Truth to tell, I think my poor Alf is a little jealous. Though I said nothing about it, he heard from the parishioners about the crowds in the church.'

'Must be awful to be a vicar and to be expected to act like a saint,' said Agatha. 'All right. I'll be there on Sunday.'

When she got back to her cottage, Agatha opened all the windows and the kitchen door as well and let her cats, Hodge and Boswell, out into the garden. I don't think they even missed me, thought Agatha, watching them roll on the warm grass. Doris comes in and feeds them and lets them in and out and they are perfectly happy with her. There was a ring at the doorbell and she went to answer it. John Armitage, her neighbour, stood there.

'I just came to welcome you back,' he said.

'Thanks,' retorted Agatha. 'Oh, well, you may as well come in and have a drink.'

She was always surprised, every time she saw him, at how good-looking he was with his lightly tanned face, fair hair and green eyes. Although he was about the same age as she was herself, his face was smooth and he looked younger, a fact that annoyed her almost as much as the fact that he had propositioned her because he had thought she would be an easy lay. He was a successful detective story writer.

They carried their drinks out into the garden. 'The chairs are a bit dusty,' said Agatha. 'Everything in the garden's dusty. So what's been going on?'

'Writing and walking. Oh, and tired to death of all the women in the village babbling about how wonderful the new curate is.'

'And is he wonderful?'

'Smarmy bastard.'

'You're just cross because you're no longer flavour of the month.'

'Could be. Haven't you seen him?'

'I haven't had time. I'm going to church on Sunday to have a look.'

'Let me know what you think. There's something wrong there.'

'Like what?'

'Can't put my finger on it. He doesn't seem quite real.'

'Neither do you,' commented Agatha rudely.

'In what way?'

'You're . . . what? Fifty-three? And yet your skin is smooth and tanned and there's something robotic about you.'

'I did apologize for having made a pass at you. You haven't forgiven me, obviously.'

'Yes, I have,' said Agatha quickly, although she had not. 'It's just . . . you never betray any emotions. You don't have much small talk.'

'I can't think of anything smaller than speculation about a new village vicar. Have you ever tried just accepting people as they are instead of as something you want them to be?'

'You mean what I see is what I get?'

'Exactly.'

What Agatha really wanted was a substitute for her ex-husband and she was often irritated that there was nothing romantic about John, but as she hardly ever thought things through, she crossly dismissed him as a bore.

'So is it possible we could be friends?' asked John. 'I mean, I only made that one gaffe.'

'Yes, all right,' said Agatha. She was about to add ungraciously that she had plenty of friends, but remembered in time that before she had moved to the Cotswolds from London, she hadn't had any friends at all.

'In that case, have lunch with me after church on Sunday.'

'Right,' said Agatha. 'Thanks.'

She and John arrived at the church on Sunday exactly five minutes before the service was due to begin and found there were no seats left in the pews and they had to stand at the back.

The tenor bell in the steeple above their heads fell silent. There was a rustle of anticipation in the church. Then Tristan Delon walked up to the altar and turned around. Agatha peered round the large hat of the woman in front of her and let out a gasp of amazement.

The curate *was* beautiful. He stood there, at the altar, with a shaft of sunlight lighting up the gold curls of his hair, his pale white skin, his large blue eyes, and his perfect mouth. Agatha stood there in a daze. Mechanically, she sang the opening hymn and listened to the readings from the Bible. Then the curate mounted the pulpit and began a sermon about loving thy neighbour. He had a well-modulated voice. Agatha listened to every word of a sermon she would normally have damned as mawkish and boring.

At the end of the service, it took ages to get out of the church. So many wanted to chat to the curate, now stationed on the porch. At last, it was Agatha's turn. Tristan gazed into her eyes and held her hand firmly.

'Beautiful sermon,' gushed Agatha.

He smiled warmly at her. 'I am glad you could come to church,' he said. 'Do you live far away or are you from the village?'

'I live here. In Lilac Lane,' gabbled Agatha. 'Last cottage.'

John coughed impatiently behind her and Agatha reluctantly moved on.

'Isn't he incredible?' exclaimed Agatha as they walked to the local pub, the Red Lion, where they had agreed earlier to have lunch.

'Humph,' was John's only reply.

So when they were seated in the pub over lunch, Agatha went on, 'I don't think I have ever seen such a beautiful man. And he's tall, too! About six feet, would you say?'

'There's something not quite right about him,' said John. 'It wasn't a sparkling sermon, either.'

'Oh, you're just jealous.'

'Believe it or not, Agatha, I am not in the slightest jealous. I would have thought that you, of all people, would not fall for a young man simply because of his looks like all those other silly women.'

'Oh, let's talk about something else,' said Agatha sulkily. 'How's the new book going?'

John began to talk and Agatha let his words drift in and out of her brain while she plotted about ways and means to see the curate alone. Could she ask for spiritual guidance? No, he might tell Mrs Bloxby and Mrs Bloxby would see through that ruse. Maybe dinner? But she was sure he would be entertained and fêted by every woman not only in Carsely, but in the villages around.

'Don't you think so?' she realized John was asking.

'Think what?'

'Agatha, you haven't been listening to a word I've said. I think I'll write a book and call it *Death of a Curate*.'

'I've got a headache,' lied Agatha. 'That's why I wasn't concentrating on what you were saying.'

After lunch, Agatha was glad to get rid of John so that she could wrap herself in brightly coloured dreams of the curate. She longed to call on Mrs Bloxby, but Sundays were busy days for the vicar's wife and so she had to bide her time with impatience until Monday morning. She hurried along to the vicarage but only Alf, the vicar, was there and he told her curtly that his wife was out on her rounds.

'I went to church on Sunday,' said Agatha. 'I've never seen such a large congregation.'

'Oh, really,' he said coldly. 'Let's hope it is still large when I resume my duties next Sunday. Now if you will excuse me . . .'

He gently closed the door.

Agatha stood there seething with frustration. Across the road from the church stood the house where Tristan had a room. But she could not possibly call on him. She had no excuse.

She was just walking away when she saw Mrs Bloxby coming towards her. Agatha hailed her with delight. 'Want to see me?' asked Mrs Bloxby. 'Come inside and I'll put the kettle on.'

Mrs Bloxby opened the vicarage door. The vicar's voice sounded from his study with dreadful clarity. 'Is that you, dear? That awful woman's just called.'

'Excuse me,' said Mrs Bloxby and darted into the study and shut the door behind her.

She emerged a few moments later, rather pink in the face. 'Poor Alf, some gypsy woman's been round pestering him to buy white heather. He's rather tetchy with the heat. I'll make tea.'

'Coffee, please.' Agatha followed her into the kitchen.

'We'll go into the garden and you can have a cigarette.'

'You forget. I've given up smoking. That trip to the hypnotist worked. Cigarettes still taste like burning rubber, the way he said they would.'

Mrs Bloxby made coffee, put two mugs of it on a tray and carried the tray out into the garden. 'This dreadful heat,' she said, putting the tray down on the garden table. 'It does make everyone so crotchety.'

'I was at church on Sunday,' began Agatha.

'So many people. Did you enjoy it?'

'Very much. Very impressed with the curate.'

'Ah, our Mr Delon. Did you see anything past his extraordinary good looks?'

'I spoke to him on the porch. He seems charming.'

'He's all of that.'

'You don't like him, and I know why,' said Agatha.

'Why?'

'Because he is filling up the church the way Mr Bloxby never could.'

'Mrs Raisin, when have I ever been *petty*?'

'Sorry, but he does seem such a wonderful preacher.'

'Indeed! I forget what the sermon was about. Refresh my memory.'

But try as she could, Agatha could not remember what it had all been about and she reddened under Mrs Bloxby's mild gaze.

'You know, Mrs Raisin, beauty is such a dangerous thing. It can slow character formation because people are always willing to credit the beautiful with character attributes they do not have.'

'You really don't like him!'

'I do not know him or understand him. Let's leave it at that.'

Agatha felt restless and discontented when she returned home. She had started to make up her face again and wear her most elegant clothes. Surely her meetings with the curate were not going to be confined to one-minute talks on a Sunday on the church porch.

The doorbell rang. Ever hopeful, Agatha checked her hair and make-up in the hall mirror before opening the door. Miss Simms, the secretary of the ladies' society, stood there.

'Come in,' urged Agatha, glad of any diversion.

Miss Simms teetered after Agatha on her high heels. Because of the heat of the day, she was wearing the minimum: tube top, tiny skirt and no tights. Agatha envied women who were able to go around in hot weather without stockings or tights. When she went bare-legged, her shoes rubbed her heels and the top of her feet and raised blisters.

'Isn't he gorgeous,' gasped Miss Simms, flopping down on a kitchen chair. 'I saw you in church.'

'The curate? Yes, he's quite something to look at.'

'He's more than that,' breathed Miss Simms. 'He's got the gift.'

'What gift? Speaking in tongues?'

'Nah! Healing. I had this terrible pain in me back and I met him in the village and told him about it. He took me round to his place and he laid his hands on my back and I could feel a surge of heat.'

284

I'll bet you could, thought Agatha, sour with jealousy.

'And the pain had gone, just like that!'

There was a clatter as Agatha's cleaner, Doris Simpson, came down the stairs carrying the vacuum cleaner. 'Just going to do the sitting-room and then I'll be off,' she said, putting her head round the kitchen door.

'We was just talking about the new curate,' said Miss Simms.

'Oh, him,' snorted Doris. 'Slimy bastard.'

'Come back here,' shouted Agatha as Doris retreated.

'What?' Doris stood in the doorway, her arms folded over her apron, Agatha's cats purring and winding their way around her legs.

'Why did you call Tristan a slimy bastard?' asked Agatha.

'I dunno.' Doris scratched her grey hair. 'There's something about him that gives me the creeps.'

'But you don't know him, surely,' complained Agatha.

'No, just an impression. Now I must get on.'

'What does *she* know about anything?' grumbled Miss Simms. 'She's only a cleaner,' she added, forgetting that she herself was sometimes reduced to cleaning houses when she was between what she euphemistically called 'gentlemen friends'.

'Exactly,' agreed Agatha. 'What's his place like?'

'Well, Mrs Feathers's cottage is ever so dark, but he's brightened up the room with pictures and throw rugs and that. He doesn't have his own kitchen, but old Mrs Feathers, she cooks for him.'

'Lucky Mrs Feathers,' said Agatha.

'I was wondering if there was any chance of a date.'

Agatha stiffened. 'He's a man of the cloth,' she said severely.

'But he ain't Catholic. He can go out with girls same as anybody.'

'What about your gentleman friend in bathroom fittings?'

Miss Simms giggled. 'He wouldn't have to know. Anyway, he's married.'

The normally pushy Agatha was beginning to feel outclassed. Besides, Tristan was young – well, maybe thirty-something, and Miss Simms was in her late twenties.

When Miss Simms had left, Agatha nervously paced up and down. She jerked open a kitchen drawer and found herself looking down at a packet of cigarettes. She took it out, opened it and lit one. Glory be! It tasted marvellous. The hypnotist's curse had gone. She hung on to the kitchen table until the first wave of dizziness had passed. Think what you're doing to your health, your lungs, screamed the governess in her head. 'Shove off,' muttered Agatha to the inner voice.

There was another ring at the doorbell.

Probably some other woman come to gloat about a laying-on of hands by the curate, thought Agatha sourly.

She jerked open the door.

Tristan stood there, smiling at her.

Agatha blinked at the vision in blue shirt and blue chinos. 'Oh, Mr Delon,' she said weakly. 'How nice.'

'Call me Tristan,' he said. 'I noticed you at church on Sunday. And I heard that you used to live in London. I'm still a city boy and still out of my depth in the country. This is very last minute, but I wondered whether you would be free to have dinner with me tonight?'

'Yes, that would be lovely,' said Agatha, wishing she had put on a thicker layer of make-up. 'Where?'

'Oh, just at my place, if that's all right.'

'Lovely. What time?'

'Eight o'clock.'

'Fine. Won't you come in?'

'Not now. On my rounds. See you this evening.'

He gave her a sunny smile and waved and walked off down the lane.

Agatha retreated to the kitchen. Her knees were trembling. Remember your age, snarled the voice in her head. Agatha ignored it and lit another cigarette while she planned what to wear. No more sensible clothes. She did not stop to consider what gossip the curate had heard that had prompted him to ask her to dinner. Agatha considered herself a very important person, which was her way of lacquering over her feelings of inferiority.

By the time she stepped out into the balmy summer evening some hours later in a gold silk dress, the bedroom behind her in the cottage was a wreck of discarded clothes. The dress was a plain shirtwaister, Agatha having decided that full evening rig would not be suitable for dinner in a village cottage.

She kept her face averted as she passed the vicarage and knocked at Mrs Feathers's door. She had not told Mrs Bloxby about the invitation, feeling that that lady would not approve.

Old Mrs Feathers answered the door. She was grey-haired and stooped and had a mild, innocent face. 'Just go on upstairs,' she said.

Agatha mounted the narrow cottage stairs. Tristan opened a door at the top. 'Welcome,' he said. 'How nice and cool you look.'

He ushered Agatha into a small room where a table had been laid with a white cloth for dinner.

'We'll start right away,' he said. He opened the door and shouted down the stairs, 'You can start serving now, Mrs Feathers.'

'Doesn't she need some help?' asked Agatha anxiously.

'Oh, no. Don't spoil her fun. She likes looking after me.' But Agatha felt awkward as

Mrs Feathers subsequently appeared carrying a heavy tray. She laid out two plates of pâté de foie gras, toast melba, a chilled bottle of wine and two glasses. 'Just call when you're ready for your next course,' she said.

Agatha sat down. Mrs Feathers spread a large white napkin on Agatha's lap before creaking off.

Tristan poured wine and sat down opposite her. 'Now,' he said, 'tell me what brings a sophisticated lady like yourself to a Cotswold village?'

Agatha told him that she had always had a dream of living in a Cotswold village. She left out the bit about taking early retirement because she did not want to refer to her age. And all the time she talked and ate, she admired the beauty of the curate opposite. He had the face of an angel come to earth with his cherubic, almost androgynous features framed by his gold curls, but his athletic, well-formed body was all masculine.

Tristan rose and called for the second course. Mrs Feathers appeared bearing tournedos Rossini, new potatoes and salad.

'Isn't Mrs Feathers an excellent cook?' said Tristan when they were alone again.

'Very,' said Agatha. 'This steak is excellent. Where did you buy it?'

'I leave all the shopping to Mrs Feathers. I told her to make a special effort.'

'She didn't pay for all this, I hope?'

'Mrs Feathers insists on paying for my food.'

Agatha looked at him uneasily. Surely an old widow like Mrs Feathers could not afford all this expensive food and wine. But Tristan seemed to take it as his due and he continued to question her about her life until the steak was finished and Mrs Feathers brought in baked Alaska.

'I've talked about nothing but myself,' said Agatha ruefully. 'I don't know a thing about you.'

'Nothing much to know,' said Tristan.

'Where were you before you came down here?'

'At a church in New Cross in London. I ran a boys' club there, you know, to get them off the streets. It was going well until I was attacked.'

'What on earth happened?'

'One of the gang leaders felt I was taking his members away. Five of them jumped me one night when I was walking home. I was badly beaten up, cracked ribs, all that. To tell the truth, I had a minor nervous breakdown and I felt a spell in the country would be just what I needed.'

'How awful for you,' said Agatha.

'I'm over it now. These things happen.'

'What made you want to join the church?'

'I felt I could help people.'

'And are you happy here?'

'I don't think Mr Bloxby likes me. I think he's a bit jealous.'

'He's a difficult man. I'm afraid he doesn't like me either.' They laughed, drawn together by the vicar's dislike of both of them.

'You were saying you had been involved in some detection. Tell me about that?'

So Agatha bragged away happily over dessert, over coffee, until, noticing it was nearly midnight, she reluctantly said she should leave.

'Before you go,' he said, 'I have a talent for playing the stock exchange. I make fortunes for others. Want me to help you?'

'I've got a very good stockbroker,' said Agatha. 'But I'll let you know.'

Somehow, she expected him to offer to walk her home, but he led the way downstairs and then stood facing her at the bottom. 'My turn next time,' said Agatha.

'I'll keep you to that.' He bent and kissed her gently on the mouth. She stared up at him, dazed. He opened the door. 'Goodnight, Agatha.'

'Goodnight, Tristan,' she said faintly.

The door shut behind her. Over at the vicarage, Mrs Bloxby's face appeared briefly at an upstairs window and then disappeared.

Agatha walked home sedately although she felt like running and jumping and cheering.

It was only when she reached her cottage that she realized she had not set a date for another dinner. She did not even know his phone number. She searched the phone book until she found a listing for Mrs Feathers. He would not be asleep already. She dialled. Mrs Feathers answered the phone. Agatha asked to speak to Tristan and waited anxiously.

Then she heard his voice. 'Yes?'

'This is Agatha. We forgot to set a date for dinner.'

There was a silence. Then he gave a mocking little laugh and said, 'Keen, aren't you? I'll let you know.'

'Goodnight,' said Agatha quickly and dropped the receiver like a hot potato.

She walked slowly into her kitchen and sat down at the table, her face flaming with mortification.

'You silly old fool,' said the voice in her head, and for once Agatha sadly agreed.

Her first feeling when she awoke the next day was that she never wanted to see the curate again. She felt he had led her on to make a fool of herself. A wind had got up and rattled through the dry thatch on the roof overhead and sent small dust devils dancing down Lilac Lane outside. She forced herself to get out of bed and face the day ahead. What if Tristan was joking with Mrs Bloxby about her? She made herself her customary breakfast of black coffee and decided to fill up the watering can and water the garden as the radio had announced a hose-pipe ban. She was half-way down the garden when she heard sirens rending the quiet of the village. She slowly put down the watering can and stood listening. The sirens swept past the end of Lilac Lane and up in the direction of the church and stopped.

Agatha abandoned the watering can and fled through the house and out into the lane. Her flat sandals sending up spirals of dust, she ran on in the direction of the vicarage. Please God, she prayed, let it not be Mrs Bloxby.

There were three police cars and an ambulance. A crowd was gathering. Agatha saw John Fletcher, the landlord from the Red Lion, and asked him, 'Is someone hurt? What's happened?'

'I don't know,' he said.

They waited a long time. Hazy clouds covered the hot sun overhead. The wind had died and all was still. Rumour buzzed through the crowd. It was the vicar, it was Mrs Bloxby, it was the curate.

A stone-faced policeman was on duty outside the vicarage. He refused to answer questions, simply saying, 'Move along there. Nothing to see.'

A white-coated forensic unit arrived. People began to drift off. 'I'd better open up,' said the publican. 'We'll find out sooner or later.'

Agatha was joined by John Armitage. 'What's going on?' he asked.

'I don't know,' said Agatha. 'I'm terrified something's happened to Mrs Bloxby.'

Then Agatha's friend, Detective Sergeant Bill Wong, came out of the vicarage accompanied by a policewoman.

'Bill!' called Agatha.

'Later,' he said. He and the policewoman went to Mrs Feathers's small cottage and knocked at the door. The old lady opened the door to them. They said something. She put a trembling hand up to her mouth and they disappeared inside and shut the door.

'There's your answer,' said John Armitage.

'It's the curate and he's dead because that ambulance hasn't moved!'